ALIENATION
OF
AFFECTIONS

ALSO BY PORTIA PORTER

Beaver vs. Beaver (Family Court, book 1)

Can You Stiff Your Divorce Lawyer? Tales of How Cunning Clients Can Get Free Legal Work, As Told By an Experienced Divorce Attorney

FAMILY COURT

BOOK 2

ALIENATION
OF
AFFECTIONS

PORTIA PORTER

CHEETAH
PRESS

Copyright © 2016 by Portia Porter

All rights reserved.

Published in the United States by Cheetah Press
Photography by Frances Twitty
Logo art by DolphyDolphiana
CHEETAH PRESS™ and the portrayal of two cheetahs with a book are trademarks of Cheetah Press

Library of Congress Application Number 1-3953262051
Porter, Portia
FAMILY COURT, Book 2 "Alienation of Affections"
visit www.porterbooks.com for updates
ISBN   978-0-997-5555-5-4
e-book ISBN 978-0-997-5555-4-7

Manufactured in the United Stated of America
10 9 8 7 6 5 4 3 2
First Edition 2016

For Valentina

TABLE OF CONTENTS

Martha Grimm Demands Service   1

Alienation of Affections   11

No Such Thing As Your Day In Court   24

Can't Make a Fruit Salad Without Cutting a Banana

                                                42

The Judge   53

The Mousetraps   63

The Game   74

The Letter   80

The Judge's Wife and The Letter   87

The Great Negotiator   94

The Goat and the Eighteen Wheeler Truck   104

The Dress   113

The Portrait by Frank Covino   120

The Epilogue   127

MARTHA GRIMM DEMANDS SERVICE

MRS. MARTHA GRIMM declared, "No divorce."

Reclining comfortably on the tufted leather of our conference room, Martha Grimm was reciting her demands: "No court. No hearings. No dividing who-gets-what in the kitchen utensils category."

She was bending her flawless fingers to underscore every "no." Her thumb, index and middle finger were now pressed comfortably together.

We nodded encouragingly.

To demonstrate complete accord, I scrupulously wrote out every requirement on my yellow legal pad in my most legible longhand, "*peaceful resolution.*"

Writing in longhand was strictly for show: on the far end of the conference table, my assistant (nicknamed The Raccoon for reasons into which he'd rather not rummage) was committing every word into a tiny Mac. Everything a client said in conference became a Morse code of hushed click-clickety-clicks: "No court, no hearings, no to the squabbling about kitchen utensils."

Clickety-click.

Click.

So far, so good. Mrs. Grimm's requests were a perfectly sensible set of marching orders. Our little law-firm had many a time and oft resolved romantic entanglements without litigation. Court is a dead end, anyhow.

I nodded again reassuringly, "No court. Can do."

But Mrs. Grimm was not finished. Her three fingers still pinched together, the ring finger started its travel to join in, "and no lawyers," she exhaled.

The click-clickety-click of transcription waned and stopped. The Raccoon's brain caught up with his typing hands, and he was staring at the screen, reading what he had just typed in, "*No lawyers.*"

"But we *are* lawy…" The Raccoon mumbled barely audibly, straining to process the implications of the just-received dictation.

Mrs. Grimm went on, "It's just a family matter. No

sense bringing lawyers into this."

Because we were a law firm, and because she did book this appointment with us and paid to seek my counsel, that final demand was somewhat unsettling.

The Raccoon, my faithful and straightforward aide, always the first to speak his mind, sprang to seek clarification.

"But then how . . . what are we . . . what do you want us to . . ."

Mrs. Grimm thrust her index finger in Raccoon's direction ever so slightly and startled him.

"No lawyers," Mrs. Grimm repeated firmly.

The Raccoon threw a bewildered glance my way, telegraphing, "*You* are the lawyer, *you* deal with this nonsense." The Raccoon always remembers that he is not the lawyer here as soon as things get weird.

"What would you like *us* to do?" I ventured. "What's your plan?"

"I want to tell my story. That's where you come in." She shrugged like it was quite obvious that our law firm was in the story-telling business.

"Tell your story to whom?" I pried with all of the diplomacy that I could muster.

"Himself! That cheating . . . Mr. Grimm. He needs to see what he has done . . ."

"See how?"

"I want my day in court," she insisted.

The hushed clicking of the transcription faltered again. The Raccoon was scrolling up his screen, squinting. Yes, he remembered it right: Mrs. Grimm had just said "no court."

"I want to hire you," finished Mrs. Grimm, her voice too sonorous for the sudden hush that had befallen the conference room, "but only if are you brave enough to take my case."

Divorcing clients always talk about bravery. Like their spouses are fire-breathing dragons and sorceresses who can turn me into a braying donkey. I shook off the "bravery" challenge and tried to concentrate. It was my turn to speak, but I felt like I had been struck dumb, dumb in both senses of the word. In my mind, I was re-playing the client's demands. *No lawyers, but she came to hire a law firm. No court, but she wants "her day in court."*

It was like one of those goat-cabbage-wolf-boat puzzles. I've never been good at those.

"Also," added Mrs. Grimm in the off-hand way one adds a chocolate bar to the pile of check-out items while waiting in line at the Barnes & Noble cashier, "One more thing I'd like you to do."

"What's that?"

"I'd like his cheating ass back. I have too much invested to cut my losses now."

4

It is not that Martha Grimm had made impossible demands. Viewed charitably, most of her demands were sensible enough, wise even.

Martha preferred to avoid the indignity of bringing a lawsuit against her husband, and that was smart.

She'd like to have her marriage back.

Who wouldn't!

"*I* wouldn't, no way," blurted The Raccoon with the wonderfully baseless self-assurance of a man laboring under the delusion that he is much more attractive than he really is, "I'd never abide."

"You are too young to understand."

"You are too ol. . .," started The Raccoon stupidly, "overly involved with the clients," he corrected himself.

Martha was not an old woman, but she was no spring chicken either. And she had never been a lover adventuress. Even back when she was twenty, new introductions bored her. Now that she was forty-two, she certainly had no taste for breaking in a new husband. Life with Mr. Grimm was comfortable, pleasant and safe. Why should Martha give it up for some little opportunistic tart? Let *her* move out of the way!

So she did not want to go to court, and wanted her

marriage back. Those demands made sense.

But, there was also Mrs. Grimm's plan to "tell her story," "to be heard," "to have her day in court." Like most people going through a divorce, Martha Grimm needed an arbiter who'd listen and confirm that she, Martha, was in the right. That she could still tell which way was up. That her life deserved a spotlight and clapping fans, and the dramatic role of the beautiful, suffering leading lady.

"I want to tell my story"—the most often ordered item on divorce lawyers' menu. Years ago, when I started out in this business, I despised this request. Who in their right mind would ask for it? Who would want to have their laundry washed in front of strangers? To a well-adjusted, happy person, this demand would appear a megalomaniac's folly. But now that I've seen a divorce or two and considered how this need comes about, I get it.

What you have to understand is that there's always a history.

It usually starts out with the cheating and the gaslighting.

To be sure, no woman is ever completely deceived by a man who looks her square in the eye and swears repeatedly, insistently, gently that the uneasy feeling which had been plaguing her for months was "Merely the atrocious weather," and that "There's just a lot going on at the office, dear," and "It's all in your head, sweetheart."

No woman is completely taken by such primitive attempts at deception. The operative word here being "completely." Most women are taken in a little, usually because they choose to be.

Martha Grimm was no exception. She knew the unpleasant truth, of course. She was not a stupid woman. Far from it! But it was nicer to believe that her mind played the tricks, not her husband. She taught herself to think that her sense of reality erred: her husband was not cheating. At first, that worked quite well, at least up to a point.

After all, they were The Grimms!

In Ducklingburg, a party became an Event if The Grimms graced it.

Mrs. Grimm was the one who announced the winners at the Daffodil Charity Auction, and Mr. Grimm was the one who steadied the trophy until the winner ran up to the scene for Mrs. Grimm to present it. Without this carefully choreographed routine, The Spring Season just could not be. The Azalea Ball was not officially open until Mr. Grimm led Mrs. Grimm in the first foxtrot of the Fall. For the Summer literary event, she relied on her more poetic half to choose the lines that she would quote from the stage. Ms. Grimm liked to preface her quoting with a little introduction: "This poem kept me awake all night," she'd claim, "so sublimely meaningful . . .." Truth be told, Mrs. Grimm had no idea of the lines that had "kept her awake" until she took the stage and read them according to her husband's aptly crafted script. Mrs. Grimm had nary a poetically sensitive brain cell in her perfectly coifed head. Mrs. Grimm had the head for business. But here too, she relied on her husband's manly charm. The men in middle management were so much more agreeable when handled by another man. Her Board knew, of course, that Mr. Grimm was not really the hand that held the reins, but it was so much easier when he came to "give her voice," as she liked to call it.

Mrs. Grimm was an exquisite woman at the charities and an iron-fisted business owner in her boardrooms, and she needed a man to frame her beauty and give her weight. She had no interest in raising her delicate voice to break up the discord in the meetings or to look for a dance partner. That last thought made her shudder. *A new man's hand on her waist . . . that was bordering on unsanitary!*

No, she preferred Mr. Grimm's familiar stewarding touch.

Of course, she was no dummy. She saw the fortune seekers at the less exclusive parties—their eyes trying to catch his; their bouncy assets trying to divert her husband's fond attentions. But surely, her husband was not looking. Or was he?

Before long, though, the mental effort of rationalizing the facts and her Pollyanna pretenses became corrosive: she started questioning her own sanity. That's when confirming that her husband was a cheater started to sound a lot better than the alternative. In the fullness of time, a woman can move on and get a new husband. Losing one's mind threatens to be a more permanent handicap.

Think that it's weak to lose one's mind over a little cheating? Imagine this scenario: you come home one night and discover your husband screwing a neighbor, right in your living room, her skinny ass catching the rainbow reflections from the crystals of your favorite chandelier. Speechless and soundless and undetected by the busily engaged couple, you retreat to your Mother's, and do not return to the house until daybreak. Over a cup of coffee, you bring up the incident, only to receive a listless, insouciant mutter in response.

"Oh no, dear, you are imagining things. Once again, a fantasy of your overactive imagination, my dear. Over-doing it with that Ambien you are taking for insomnia. It's a hypnotic drug, known to cause hallucinations. Maybe you should go see Dr. Schultz; I'll make an appointment?"

Makes a girl want validation, want to "tell her story," to a believing audience doesn't it?

Now does that "day on court" request make more sense?

Of course, the "day in court" is not always that well-intentioned. There is more than one reason that this particular dish is selected from the menu. There is the revenge of orchestrating a public humiliation of the Ex. That plays a part sometimes. There's the grab for money, power, or social relations, especially if the story involves cheating.

A scorned wife on the lugubrious mission to expose her cheating husband and "have her day in court" might have many ill-advised reasons for this drab task. But one of her reasons is decent—the desire to be sure that her own mind is not failing her. This need to tell "your story" is neither vanity or narcissism. It is simply a sanity check.

There was only one problem with Mrs. Grimm's demand for "a day in court": we could not meet it.

Nobody could.

Unfortunately, there is no such thing as "your day in court." At least, not in the sense that Martha wanted it.

We told Mrs. Grimm that we'd be in touch.

ALIENATION OF AFFECTIONS

BY OFFICE PROTOCOL (implemented after an unfortunate incident which The Raccoon would rather not discuss) no new contestant was accepted as a client of the firm until the entire firm voted on it.

There were four of us altogether: The indefatigable and brave Raccoon and his shadow Hoppy attended to the legwork of the practice. The Management—a strict but unfair ruler—counted the money and always found it lacking. My job, as the only one with the law license, was to attend to the nebulous demands of the Law. I was pretty sure that the other three on my crew thought that they could do better without me, if only the capricious state laws of South Duck stopped making practicing law without a license illegal, an actual crime.

The transcript of the meeting with Mrs. Grimm was printed in four-plicate and spread around the round glass garden table. Hoppy and The Raccoon selected that table to be our voting place because of its democratic shape, a shape that banished any head-and-foot hierarchy. Architecture has a much more meaningful hand in governance than most people consciously realize. Apparently, these two had picked up on it somehow, perhaps schooled by observing The Management's penchant to seize the dominant position at a table if such a position there be.

The Raccoon took the initiative and highlighted a few parts of the Martha Grimm meeting transcript in green for "like" and yellow for "dislike."

The vote had begun.

Of course, whatever the powers of the round garden table, our office manager had veto power, so you could say that the system was rigged.

"Will she pay?" asked The Management.

That was the only question The Management ever really cared about. Now that I think about it, those were usually the only words she ever uttered in our voting conferences. Until, that is, she'd sometimes announce, "we are declining this client, and that is final." Those words of doom were what ended it for most of the applicants to our client list.

But Mrs. Grimm would not be declined on the ground of ability-to-pay or, indeed, any other red flag. Martha Grimm was an excellent client: well-mannered, prompt, well-groomed, soft-spoken, and prepared to pay. She had requested that we give her representation and we would be fools to say no . . . if only we could solve the mystery of exactly what it was that she wanted us to do.

"Opposed?"

The Raccoon cleared his throat, "What exactly can we do for her? She needs a film crew, not a law firm," he blurted out.

The Management swiveled on her chair and gave him a withering look.

"No, really," insisted The Raccoon, his cue to shut it having been valiantly ignored. "She wants a day in court, but no court? She wants to tell her story. Hire a film crew. They'll tell it all right."

The Management disengaged from staring down The Raccoon, and swiveled back forty-five degrees to her left, to redirect her query to the only lawyer in the room.

"*What* is he talking about?" she asked me.

"Mrs. Grimm has a few unusual requests," I began to explain.

"She said she wants 'his cheating ass back,'"

interjected The Raccoon.

I nodded my accord and explained the list of things that were a "no" on Mrs. Grimm's list—no lawyers, no divorce and no court.

The Management chewed those revelations over briefly.

"Why no court?"

Incorrigible Raccoon pressed his finger to the last page of the meeting transcript, a page which he had mostly covered in yellow (for "dislike") highlighter.

"*A lady* does not take her cheating husband to court," he read in high voice, meant to imitate Mrs. Grimm's notably stilted, proper manner of speaking.

"The lady wants to have her day in court, but she does not want to sue her husband?" summed up The Management.

The Raccoon and I nodded affirmatively in unison.

"What's the problem?"

"We can't have a day in court with nobody to sue," I said the obvious, "and, nonetheless, 'a lady does not sue her husband'. Says so right here, in the notes."

The Management did not miss one beat, "Does a lady sue a floozy who stole her husband? What does it say in the notes about *that*?"

An alienation of affections suit! Of course!

In some parts of America, the affections of a spouse are considered to be property, protected by the law from theft in much the same ways as all the other stuff one owns—cars, houses, cash or dogs. Those stealing the affections of a married person are forced to compensate the cuckolded spouse for the value of the stolen commodity. The price which thieves might be ordered to pay can even amount to millions of dollars. Affections get expensive.

The State of South Duck had not seen an alienation of affections lawsuit in twenty-five years, but the law was still on the books. Even if in a sad state of neglect in South Duck, alienation of affections suits were all the rage in some States close by. A scorned wife in North Carolina had just won a fifteen-million-dollar award, stirring up another blast of loud debates over the proper role, if any, of this legal doctrine in 21st-century family law. Every divorce lawyer's blog had an opinion. Liberals and the feminists insisted that the law was retrograde and should be abolished. After all, they said, a man is not really a woman's possession and "stealing affections" objectifies him. And a woman is definitely not anybody's possession, and the feminists had proved that with years of loud parades.

But the conservatives put the law on their banner and waved the "family values" battle cry. Conservatives insist that the scorned wife's right to sue her husband's mistress validates family values. Floozies of this world stole from the honest women, and there should be appropriate retribution in hard cash.

Both camps were vocal to a shrill.

"Where do you stand on the law?" asked Hoppy after he grasped the idea that being "the other woman" could carry a multi-million-dollar price-tag.

"It's perfectly valid," I said, referring only to its enforceability in South Duck. It is pointless to argue whether the law is good or bad. As the cliché correctly asserts, "it is what it is."

"That's nifty to know," mused Hoppy, "in case my spouse cheats, I already know what to do."

"You couldn't even get a date for this weekend," countered The Raccoon. "And men get sued too, you know." That made Hoppy consider changing camps.

"I read on the internet that the alienation of affections law protects the children," well-informed Raccoon chimed in.

I was not clear how any person's children could get helped by a lawsuit that drags one of their parents in the mud and forces a recounting of every act of infidelity in graphic words and under oath. And maybe even full-color porn video from the covert surveillance camera? But I was not going to argue.

The proponents of the law also believe that it "sends a message" to the "home wreckers." But, there are no statistics to tell us for sure whether the home-wreckers get that message. Are there fewer home-wreckers in

Illinois, where the law is still alive and well than, say, in New York, where the law is abolished? Has anybody ever sent a SurveyMonkey question around Chicago, asking: "If they abolish the alienation of affections law, would you be more likely to sleep with your married boss? Please mark only one that applies:

    A. Agree completely
    B. Agree somewhat
    C. Disagree completely
    D. What law? I've been screwing my married boss for a year just to get promoted. *Now* you're telling me there's a law?!"

The Raccoon sneaked away from the round table, and was busy googling for fellow divorce lawyers' opinions. He found a quote: "This Rosen fellow says 'the law just polarizes everyone and devastates everything in its path including the children and both spouses.'"

The Management snorted indignantly: "Like they all would have lived as one big happy family, but the alienation of affections law barged in and snuffed out the spirit of marital bliss! Ha!"

"The jury awards are in the millions," read The Raccoon.

With her usual unwavering eye on the financial implications to our firm, The Management decided,

"This Floozy destroyed a perfectly good marriage. The Grimms would have screeched their way through a rough patch, and then lasted harmoniously till death did them part. Clearly. We'll be on the side of the angels here."

"How do we know that?" asked Hoppy. The innate resilience of romance was always a topic with Hoppy.

"We represent the Wife, do we not? The Wife told us that it's a good marriage, did she not?"

"What if we represented the mistress?"

"Some couples are miserable together. Liberating a husband from a bad union is sometimes a favor to the innocent partner. Not every adulterous lover destroys a good marriage."

"It's all relative," summed up The Raccoon, regaining his stride.

"To what?" was slow Hoppy.

"To who our client is," was Raccoon's professional response.

"Exactly. Let's present this golden opportunity to Mrs. Grimm," decided The Management, "What's next on our agenda today?"

When Martha Grimm discovered how the law of

alienation of affections worked, it was love at first sight.

"It is a Godsend! I'll have a day in court without taking my husband to court!"

She loved everything about suing her competitor. She'd show up the floozy, she said. She'd prove to all that she was not crazy. Her husband was a cheat; she did not make that up. In court, it would all come out. And—she was absolutely sure of it—she'd get her husband back. She knew that he'd come crawling back just as soon as she had the chance to *tell her story*. When the drama was played out as Martha hoped, the villainess would be suitably punished while the leading lady and her errant—but now repentant—husband would live Happily Ever After.

In my professional experience, none of that plan stood the chance of a snowball in Hell.

———————

"About your day in court," I said. "I have some unfortunate news."

"Oh?"

"There is no such thing as a day in court. Not the way it is dramatized on TV, anyhow."

We were back in the conference room again. The Raccoon stopped typing because he already knew the next stretch by heart.

Since "I want my day in court" is the most requested item on the divorce lawyer's menu, I've developed a standard response: there is no such thing.

In my repertoire of soliloquies delivered to the clients, the one that's used the most is "There's no such thing as *your* day in court." Everybody at the office can lip-synch my spiel. The Raccoon had considered putting it on the website, but was shot down by The Management. I am with The Raccoon, though. It gets repetitive. One day, I might start distributing a brochure instead. On the other hand, The Management's argument that the spiel "counts as billable time" is irrefutable.

————

If you are over a certain age, or if you just enjoy old movies, you may remember the long-running TV series *Dallas* and the long-suffering fictional wife of fictional oil baron J. R. Ewing, the beautiful Mrs. Sue Ellen Ewing.

Considered as a husband, Mr. J.R. Ewing was plainly an abject failure. Even J.R.'s own Wikipedia page dubs him "covetous, egocentric, manipulative and amoral, with psychopathic tendencies." Not the qualities that make a prized life-companion. Like many women married to cheating egocentrics, Mrs. Ewing became understandably unhappy with her marriage.

Neglected, manipulated and humiliated for a dozen of seasons straight, Sue Ellen dealt with her marital misfortunes in creative ways. She slept with her husband's sworn enemy, consulted a psychologist, and took to drinking. Nothing helped until Sue Ellen finally worked up the nerve to leave.

One of the reasons it took Mrs. Ewing such a long time to pull the plug on her marriage was also as old as the Freud's pipe adage: the abuse and manipulation (together with a dash too much of various alcoholic beverages) eroded Sue Ellen's sense of self and made her question her own view of reality.

Was J.R. really a monster, she wondered, or was the marital strife somehow her own fault? Should she leave, or was the answer to stay and just try a little bit harder?

In short, like many women married to cheating, manipulative egocentrics, Sue Ellen was a woman unsure of what her story really was. Psychologists might diagnose her as a victim of "gaslighting," a form of psychological abuse in which a victims are manipulated into doubting their own memory, perception and sanity. To rebuild herself, Sue Ellen needed to "tell her story." She had to have adequate proof that she was in fact the victim, that her husband was the villain, and that the demise of her marriage was (largely) not her fault. Plus, she needed proof that she was not crazy.

All this should start to sound very familiar.

But here is where it diverges: Mrs. Ewing's approach to "telling her story" was *not* to seek her "day in court." Instead, Mrs. Ewing did something different: *Mrs. Ewing told her story in a movie.* Literally!

———————

Sue Ellen Ewing hit upon the only practical way to deal with the problem.

She did not testify in court and did not hire fancy lawyers to have her husband cross-examined in front of God and everybody. Instead, she made a different investment.

She bought herself a movie studio.

The full might of her shrewdly purchased entertainment empire was marshalled to create her life story, her own uncontradicted version of reality.

A hot Hollywood writer was hired to adapt Sue Ellen's meticulous diary into the movie's script and, incidentally, to romance Sue Ellen. This way, he was able to probe the subject more intimately.

Sue Ellen personally sifted through a crowd of actors auditioning for the role of her husband—the role that called for depicting a charming but villainous and ultimately unlovable rascal.

She also found a professional to portray her own essence—an actress as elegant as Sue Ellen and just as beautiful and, what's more, ten years younger.

And when every last detail of her story was put perfectly together, Sue Ellen assembled her audience. She, the scorned wife, and J.R. Ewing, the offending husband, came alone and sat side by side in the entirely empty theater. Sue Ellen cued the projectionist to, "Roll!" and her cinematic masterpiece lit up the screen.

And that is how Sue Ellen dealt with the need to "tell her story."

She wrote it, she produced it, she sifted through the actors, she captured her audience, and she had it played, all exactly the way she wanted it.

Unfortunately, not even throwing a lot of money at a highly skilled legal team can provide a wronged spouse with anywhere near as satisfying experience as Sue Ellen's.

NO SUCH THING AS YOUR DAY
IN COURT

IF YOU HAVE ever gone through breakup and divorce, you probably have said these words to yourself: "I've got to write a book about it." Most of my female clients and at least half of my male clients have said these words. But, to my knowledge, none of them went through with it.

Instead, American housewives choose the courthouse as a forum to tell their story. In modern America, "your day in court" is viewed (and often used interchangeably) with the opportunity to "tell your story." Many a client has said to me: "I want my story told, I want my day in court, I do not care how much it costs, I want the truth to come out."

But why, best efforts notwithstanding, will the drama produced in a courtroom inevitably be doomed to not work out anywhere near as well as Sue Ellen's adroitly staged movie?

———————

If you have never been a part of a court performance before, there are a couple of things you need to consider quite soberly. You will indeed have a chance to tell "your story," but there will be a few obstacles. Some might prefer to call them "hopelessly frustrating barriers" rather than mere obstacles.

First, there's *the narrative*. Sue Ellen's hired writer took particular care to faithfully craft the script that preserved Sue Ellen's own vision; Sue Ellen's private diaries served as the polar star to guide the script writer in the application of his storytelling craft. You'd want the same. If you want a day in court, a day to tell your story, then control over the script is critical. You do not have a script writer, but you do have a lawyer who, without a doubt, will take stringent care to create the desired narrative, the script that will faithfully reflect your own voice and vision. You'll see it in rehearsals, I mean the court prep where you and your witnesses (your supporting cast) have a run-through of the questions and suggested answers. So far so good.

But the limitations of the court will come into play as soon as you step through the door. Turns out, while your lawyer was working on your script, your spouse's lawyer was busy working on your spouse's script, and now you are basically involved in the production of a film with two conflicting scripts, two antagonistic show runners, and a stable of amateur actors who constantly go off script and defy the show-runners' instructions.

In the end, your narrative will look like somebody is switching between two TV channels, alternating between an HBO comedy and an ABC dramedy.

Speaking of *the actors*. You may remember that Sue Ellen was particularly careful in casting just the right guy to play her husband? The guy who'd be handsome but villainous; charming enough to account for her fall, but not so charming as to steal the limelight from her suffering; ripe to portraying the insidious destruction she suffered and—the hardest of all—the character in the narrative whom the audience would eagerly learn to hate. After sifting through scores of suitors, the perfect actor to play slimy JR in his wife's movie was found at last. And make no mistake about this one—the perfect actor is the making of the perfect play, the *sine qua non*.

Instead, when you come to court, you unfortunately have none of the benefits of this careful casting. In court, you are stuck with the only choice of actor to play your spouse: your own spouse.

You might be wondering: but what's the problem? What's wrong with the original? Isn't that the closest to the truth? Doesn't art imitate life?

Yes.

Sort of.

What art imitates is the *essence* of life. Cleverly selected features are rendered more pronounced in good art. Motives are made more clear, colors more vibrant. That's an artsy answer.

Or, to put it more bluntly, your spouse is a liar, intent to conceal his evil nature, to tune down the rottenness, or even completely mask it. I suspect you know already that your spouse will turn on the charm, and sprinkle so much pixy dust that even the courtroom bailiff will sneeze.

Casting the villain—or villainess, as the case may be—is tricky enough in the movies and books where the director has complete creative control and as many rewrites as it takes to get things just right. But in court, where the "villain" is resisting that characterization and you only have one take, framing the villain satisfactorily becomes almost mission impossible.

And yet, that mission pales in difficulty when you

think of casting the main character—YOU.

In case you are puzzled by this point, consider an actual movie set. If you were a celebrity and they'd shoot a story of your life, would you come and play yourself opposite a famous Hollywood star? Of course not, don't be silly! You'd get a professional, so everything looks tip-top. And that's nothing to feel bad about either. Actors themselves get doubles, and not just the stunt doubles for those tricky times when the script calls for jumping off the cliff. Actors get doubles for every movie part.

Inferior butt?

Get a double.

Legs could be longer?

Double again.

Rumor has it, Julia Roberts got a double for parts of her body in the Pretty Woman film, and for the *entire* Pretty Woman poster. The *entire* body. Supposedly, only the head is actually hers. (Look up Shelley Michelle if that revelation is hard to swallow.) It's easy to find a body double, too. An actress client of mine lists as a credit a role of buttocks and legs of a very popular actress whose name remains semi-confidential. The world is just a better place when everybody specializes in doing what they are best at. Some people are true artists. Some have amazing butts. But again, we digress.

If your life were a movie, of course, the perfectly

fitted professional thespian would be located to convey your essence and, indeed, maybe even to improve upon it a bit. And there also would be the flattering wardrobe, and the makeup, and the lighting. There would be the retouch for the posters, and the doubles for the body parts of your double.

Yes, you read it right.

There would be an acting professional to play you. And then there might also be stand-ins to depict any body part whatsoever that doesn't deliver quite the desired effect.

And—let's be completely honest here—anyone who portrays you (or any of your parts) would have to be twenty pounds lighter and ten years younger in order to most advantageously capture your essence. Young enough to fit your wedding attire, but poised enough to depict sympathetically your calmest, most stage-stealing moments. That's the casting strategy that Sue Ellen chose so calculatingly and shrewdly to follow. There's no shame in that. If twenty-two year-old Julia Roberts was thought to need a body double, would you really want to take a chance on your own tired old body??

In a movie, defects—of appearance, of voice, or of mannerism—that detract from your desired image are no problem. Your professionally projected essence will not have to worry about breaking out into nervous scaly rash or developing a tic on the left eyelid, or hiccups, or coarse and squeaky voice, or unruly hair, or needing to go potty in the middle of the hearing. The makeup, wardrobe, the team of actors chosen to play your feet and hands and back, and the many, many takes of each scene would take care of all the unpleasant life contingencies and imperfections. And in the end, the depiction of your essence would be perfect, just as perfect as it could be and should be.

And that is the litany of the many factors to be taken into consideration in telling your story properly. Obviously, when you are in real-life court, you have to get along without the necessary tools to plaster over the weak spots in the exposition of your story. In court, you have to play yourself, and that's harder than anything else—even for professional actors who perchance wind up in a witness chair. If you are like most people, you have no acting training, and you will have little to no guidance. On top of that, the wardrobe will be limited, the makeup will be amateurish, and the lighting . . . have you seen the courtroom lighting? Do not start me on the courtroom lighting. Well, on second thought, maybe just a few words.

If any of the divorcing couples ever had second thoughts about staying together, seeing each other in courtroom lighting would put them to an emphatic halt.

If you feel nervous, you will look like you are lying.

If you get upset, your eyes will swell and you'll look like you'd been drinking.

And in any event, you will look haggard and ten years older. *Playing the protagonist* in court is a demanding and unrewarding mission.

And then, of course, there's the supporting cast. Remember Sue Ellen's supporting cast—JR's family, Sue Ellen's murderous sister and poisonous mother, all chosen and trained with one goal in mind—to shield and prop up the protagonist. That supporting cast was important too. And what do you get in court for the supporting cast? You get "your" witnesses, of course, but they never rehearse, rarely care very much about their roles, and often do not properly look the part. Under harsh cross-examination by the opposing lawyer, they will protect themselves at your expense. Sometimes they do not even bother to show up.

And all that amateurish circus is in the loose control of one overstrained show-runner—your lawyer. Best case, he's got himself a few assistants. And, by the way, how much experience does your lawyer have in actually preparing and conducting a courtroom trial and all that it entails? I raise that question because the answer might surprise you: many divorce lawyers are primarily "paper-filers" rather than "litigators" with courtroom experience. Suffice it to say, Sue Ellen's movie was not entrusted to a novice director with little theatrical experience.

When you consider all these limitations, you have to admit to yourself the truth: your day in court will simply not ever amount to much of the kind of show that you really had hoped for.

All that is a pretty upsetting perspective, but that's not where it ends.

Even if—against all odds—you managed to be the poised and elegant hero, and your lawyer managed to cross-examine your spouse into the most villainous villain, and all of your witnesses got efficiently herded and none of them went bonkers, or puked on the stand, or sold you out, and—also against all odds and defying all towering hurdles, you managed to orchestrate a show worthy of the third quarter of Pretty Woman—even if you managed to do all that, you still have something to fear: **The Audience**.

Remember Sue Ellen? She took pains at creating the perfect viewing experience for the perfect audience—a dark empty theater that allowed not a hint of distraction to her captive audience—Sue Ellen's husband sitting in the dark, soaking up every scene with mounting horror. After all, who would not pay attention to a movie co-starring oneself, even if in the role of villain?

Sue Ellen successfully contrived exactly the right result once again. But will you?

What do you have for an audience? Who will view

the characters, judge the plot, and ultimately write the critique of your show?

Many divorcing people seem to think that their spouse *is* the audience, but that is not exactly right: the spouse does not have any say-so about the final write-up.

In court, your sole audience of any importance is the judge. And the judge is a lot less interested in your "story" than you might think.

That's right.

Believe it or not, you are not the only thing on the judge's mind. The judge, distracted by the workings of his courtroom, answering his emails as he half-listens to you, worrying about his gout and his appellate record, and—let's face it—viewing your case as nothing but one of the identical gazillion and a half of cases he's heard since the day when he still remembered why he took the job—*that* judge. That judge is the reason you are producing this whole show. That judge will decide whether your show is a resounding hit, a dismal flop, or—as it often happens—a mediocrity—something in-between.

It would have been different if divorce courts had juries. Then, you'd likely be the only show that the jurors had ever seen. You'd be fresh and important and the focus of a civic duty. But you got yourself a judge for the audience. The judge expects that your movie is basically a "remake," that he's seen your movie before, over and over *ad nauseam*. He does not need to watch attentively to know how the plot goes and how it ends. Most of the time, his decision is made up three minutes after the curtain rises.

So there you have it, your day in court. Your day in court is six hours in which you get to "tell your story." The villain will fight for the hero's part, your own hero's face will break out and your hair will fall dull and unruly; the lighting will be devastating; the supporting cast will testify disappointingly or go missing; the show runner will get frantic or apathetic; and the script writer will be uninspired, inaccurate and unprofessional. And on top of that, your audience will resent you because your story is what separates your audience from the coveted drive home, the dinner and the real movie with good writing and pretty people.

Now that you know all that, can you honestly say that a trip to court will accomplish the goal of "telling your story?" Do you really get to "tell your story" if it's told chaotically and nobody really listens anyway? I don't know. It's a little like the tree falling in the empty forest dilemma.

———————

"So you see now that you should not go to court. Not if *telling your story* is the goal," I finished triumphantly. Nobody in their sound mind could want to use the courts to "tell their story." It simply does not work.

I pride myself on telling the client when she'd be a fool to waste money on our services. That is not my best quality as far as our Management is concerned. But The Management is wrong to worry. Fortunately for our bottom line, the clients never listen.

"I'd still like to hire you," responded Mrs. Grimm.

"Even though you know I think you shouldn't?"

"You'll just do your job, honey," Mrs. Grimm reached out to pat my hand, but missed. I hate it when clients pat my hand or call me "honey."

"You'll just do your job, honey, and let me do mine. We'll show Mr. Grimm what he has done."

She set sail out of the conference room door, leaving on the table a money envelope crafted in heavyweight cotton with geometric shapes in subdued gold. Mrs. Grimm was a lady, and when ladies pay the hired help, ladies place their checks in tactful envelopes.

Her hand on the door handle, thin handkerchief protecting her fingers, she looked back in and delivered an afterthought,

"And you remember, I want his cheating ass back home." She smiled sweetly and was gone, leaving behind a faint scent of expensive shampoo and the sight of my head shaking in wonderment.

The Raccoon was by my side of the table, examining the contents of the envelope. "A certified check for twenty-five thousand dollars," he noted approvingly. "Good start. But to get her husband back? How are you going to pull off this Cinderella story?"

Unlike divorce cases which are heard only by a judge (a so-called "bench trial"), a suit for alienation of affections allows for a jury trial. That means twelve pairs of eyes trapped in a box, with nothing to do all day but scrutinize the marital dirty laundry on display. If it gets heated enough or lurid enough, the trial might even attract attention from a local news crew. Maybe even TV reports videotaped on the courtroom steps.

Alienation of affections trials have a certain flourish rivalled only, perhaps, by that of trials for murder. It is a splashy cause of action.

"Not the sort of thing I'd recommend if you are in witness protection," summarized The Management, "But Mrs. Grimm did require 'to be heard'?"

"We can't win this," I said with habitual gloom, "Nobody can."

"We are not paid to win," returned The Management, "we are paid for orchestrating 'her day in court.'"

"The stupidest request ever made."

"I've seen dumber," said The Management in her usual intervention to have the last word.

———

I will spare you the boring account of how I and my minions ran up oodles of billable hours preparing to present Martha's story within the strictures of a family law courtroom setting. Better by far that we just skip ahead to when the great day finally arrived.

Showtime!

On the first day of jury selections, the courtroom was carved up like a battlefield. On the right, closest to the still empty jury box, was our campground and the trenches. The Raccoon was setting out the paper artillery. We chose the "technology courtroom," equipped with a row of tiny TV screens—one per each juror. An exhibit placed on the overhead projector would simultaneously appear with a flick of a switch on the jurors' screens. At least, that was the theory. In practice, something about the transfer from our Apple equipment to the techno-courtroom's native Windows did not take and was glitching. The Raccoon performed the required exorcism with the ritual resolve of a pre-reform priest.

Hoppy was moping around pretending to be useful.

Hoppy's official task was to "keep the record"—transcribe every word and sound uttered in court by witnesses, lawyers, the judge, and the judge's secretary, bailiffs, and any stray soul who so much as made a grunting noise out-loud.

Officially, the judge's secretaries were required to start a digital recording and record every sound of the court, then create a copy of the disc for anyone who asked. But we've had trouble in the past: most interesting parts of the recording came scratched, unintelligible or just plain inexplicably missing.

Once, when a judge's appointed Receiver made a full on the record confession of inappropriately threatening a witness, the original disc recording of the court disappeared altogether. The contrite secretary later sent out a group e-mail: she forgot to press the "record" button. She is sorry. Oops. True to my suspicious character, I saw collusion and a cover-up, and thereafter assigned Hoppy to precautionary "record duty." His job was to type. Also, he was to keep a vigilant eye on the opposition.

But there was as yet no record to be kept and no opposition to eye: neither Floozy nor her lawyer had arrived.

The lone figure in the Floozy's corner was Mr. Grimm—an urbane, impeccably dressed gentleman whose wandering affections had launched the battle. Overdressed for his part, Mr. Grimm sat conspicuously in the middle of the Floozy's left field. He was aligned on her side, in a show of support to his mistress. Distasteful!

Mrs. Grimm arrived next, dressed modestly but thoughtfully in a perfectly fitted little dusty rose dress draped over with a made-to-measure wool crepe swing jacket that flattered her tummy and softened her eyes. Every line and seam of the ensemble was in its proper place, moving with her body like they were all born together. Mrs. Grimm took her place on The Raccoon's right hand, landing lightly on her skirt with no apparent concern for garment care. She did not check her chair for specks of dust, nor pull on her hem to protect from the errant crease, nor push up her midline to spare the unseemly stretch. None of those busy little gestures— the tics which betray the common herd in their unaccustomed Sunday best—were part of Mrs. Grimm's life. Watching her take her seat in the courtroom, one knew right off, even if one did not know exactly how the impression emerged, that Mrs. Grimm had been rich for a long, long time.

"Who makes the skirt?" beauty-conscious Hoppy,

forgetting his trial duties under the spell of the textile splendor, scribbled in a note passed to me.

"*What is couture* for many thousands of $$," I scribbled back, "Get back to work."

Still looking for the magic brand that so stylishly fits the body, Hoppy pushed the note back, with underlined "who makes?"

"It's made-to-measure," The Raccoon hissed back without turning his head.

I stirred in an effort to stop the hushed squabble before Mrs. Grimm could notice, but there was no danger: her eyes were glued to a new arrival and a different sort of sartorial display: in the wake of the opposing counsel—a courthouse regular nicknamed The Great Negotiator—was The Floozy, the Defendant in this case, sashaying in with a style that contrasted starkly with that of our client, the wronged Mrs. Grimm.

The Floozy was the right age for a cheap flirtation: twice younger than Mrs. Grimm. Her gait was light and there was an air of optimism about the way she moved her body. She was brisk but smooth, like a chipmunk on her way to raid a rose garden.

The Floozy had not much experience with money before she met the Grimms. But now that she took Mr. Grimm as a lover, her shopping power jumped up to limitless, or at least she had not yet reached the limit. For the occasion of the day, she had been propped up by all the buying power of Amex Platinum, a card bestowed upon her by Mr. Grimm but which, unbeknownst to The Floozy, listed both Grimms as its account owners. The Floozy had treated the card as her own for a while now, and brought the clothes to prove it.

"Brought" being the operative word. The new clothes, the entire new life with Mr. Grimm was like a trophy. She carried it around—a point of pride for her and of object of jealousy for all of her girlfriends. Still, this new life did not feel like *hers*, no matter how hard she tried. The stupid lawsuit was the culprit, she'd determined. She just had to wait until it was won and behind her. Then her real life would start.

CAN'T MAKE A FRUIT SALAD
WITHOUT CUTTING A BANANA

SECURE IN HER perfectly versatile figure, The Floozy had never struggled with a dressing choice before. She did not boast much curve, but she had something far better, as far as the designers and the tailors were concerned: a tall leanness that could be draped to almost any shape. "Best model is a hanger, ma'am," tailors joke among themselves, "no form it couldn't take." Her best feature was a taut tan belly, which she was wont to show off in her signature look—boyish hip-height jeans and cut-off shirts.

Even the cheap, stretchy, one-cut-fits-all-mediums dresses she could afford in her pre-Mr. Grimm life had never dwarfed or uglied her. The artless construction of off-the-rack clothing had bent to her form and flattered by contrast, like an exotic rosebud would stand out stunningly from a florist's cheap standard vase. Her body shone through the cheap fabric and Mr. Grimm could not help the impulse to pluck this long-stemmed rosebud and fit it into a fully deserving vase.

Hence, the Amex Platinum in all its limitless power—a feeling as new and intoxicating as flying without gravity. The strain of fashion decision-making was also new, and not nearly as liberating. Grown-up occasions did not come up often in Floozy's life. Her life experience had not adequately endowed her with expertise in choosing the right "look" for attendance at undesirable events. Up until this day, shopping was a thing of frolic. Indeed, as the court date approached, she did not even bother checking in her closet. She knew that solid and serious was not hiding anywhere in her wardrobe. The Floozy procrastinated for a time, then headed for the mall, the presentable section.

She'd always had fun in malls. She did not mind carrying the piles of clothes to try on—it only made her step spring more and her eyes shine with anticipation. The half-naked sprints for a different size were never a bother. Even the harsh neon of the dressing room bounced off her taut skin without any notable damage to its allure. Yes, The Floozy loved to shop for clothes. But on the court clothes' shopping day, everything was changed and she was perplexed to find herself on hitherto unfamiliar terrain.

She started the quest in the Northern part of the mall, on the seventh floor where the diffusion line of Armani flanked the dedicated cashier, a clothing line designed to trap up the less worthy class of customers in its cheapened charm. By chance, she pressed on, entering the *sanctum sanctorum* of the label nestled discreetly behind the help, protected in a three-walled enclosure.

The gapingly uninhabited section dedicated to business and formal wear was the domain of a single sales consultant, whose eagle eye spotted Floozy from the very first moment that she materialized on the sales floor. The salesperson at once dropped her pastime of helping a nude male torso to get decent, and sprinted at the highest speed that her Fluevog's four-inch heeled Estellas and the store's solemn decorum allowed. Floozy was the first real prospect of the morning in the staid business wear section.

The store's young fashion consultant was an energetic girl despite her body type that was, decidedly and textbook-like, in the form of an apple. Indeed, she was a triumph of the sphere shape. Her torso widened at the waist, and the gentle curve of the hips completed the illusion that her body was drawn on an apple fruit. Her arms, though visibly firm, were plump and each joint appeared rounded, and even her palms looked like the petals of apple flowers. Her chestnut hair was pulled away from a smiling, freakishly round face and braided into a short curvy apple stem ending in tight teal-colored floppy bow, shaped like two leaves.

The girls in Alteration nicknamed her Apple Blossom, the very day that she had first arrived. In Apple's presence, one could almost smell the scent of fresh apples.

"When is the D-day?" inquired Apple Blossom, and was relieved to learn it was tomorrow. That imminent necessity meant that a purchase would be made today. It was just a question of the price.

The Blossom started to assess the situation. Her line of questions was well-tested: "Is there a special event? What is it? How formal should we go?" Her light-blue Estella heels clicked to underscore the urgency.

The Floozy tried to answer without talking about having been summoned to court as a Defendant, but circumvention was not her forte. She felt trapped.

Was it the stress of the occasion, or the unfamiliarity of the formal wear? The somber-colored clothes were forbidding. She touched the fabric, and sneaked a sniff. It even smelled expensive, but she could not imagine even trying them on. It was the sort of clothes that made one look square and crushed the spirit! The Floozy had to admit that this time, she was in no mood for shopping.

In the soul-less business dress section of the store, it hit her: *I'm buying a dress to wear for being sued. I'm actually being sued. Even after I managed to get rid of the wife, this woman is sucking all the fun out of life. Now she'll have me dressing like . . . like . . . I work for her.*

I'll never get this woman out of my life, a little voice went off in Floozy's head. She glanced around in despair, hoping for quick buy-and-dash, but each outfit was duller than its neighbor. She could not bear the humiliation . . . and that's when she saw it.

———————

The Dress was perched on a life-like mannequin— a realistic woman with exaggeratedly curvy body and inhumanly wide smile. The Dress was feminine and inviting, the first sexy thing in this land of corporate doom. And, what's more, it was familiar, as if she'd seen it before. It evoked warm remembrances of a good day, the way one looks at family photo from ages ago and sees so much more than what's actually there in the picture.

"This one! I want this one!" she pointed at the display, and next thing she knew, the mannequin sporting a 3D rack and an inhumanly thin waist was stripped naked, but still grinning just as widely and unashamedly. In due course, the scene shifted to the soft music of the changing room wherein Floozy's own reflection appeared in the three-surface mirrors.

"Do you prefer your fit this way?" inquired The Apple Blossom, and The Floozy sensed there was a hidden meaning to the question. This much was clear. But what?

"What do *you* think?" The Floozy returned the question, admiring the stitching of the silk liner.

"Oh, it's *your* taste that matters," cooed Apple Blossom, glancing over The Floozy like maybe there was a secret, but one that she was not telling.

———

Despite the hilarious curves and the apple scent, young Apple Blossom had ambition. Sure, this new position in the store was strictly sales, but she was studying to be much more, to market a line of her very own dress designs.

The online fashion design classes started with the basics: define the body type for which you're cutting the wear. That's what they said, "cutting."

Once she had seen the diagrams, she could not un-see them: *every woman was a fruit.* Her first month of classes, walking through the mall, Apple Blossom was tagging the shoppers speeding by her.

Licking an ice-cream cone, a fresh crunchy young *apple*, just like her.

Prada bag and emeralds were so lost on this old and haggard *pear*, who is trying to squeeze herself into a pencil skirt—never going to happen, no matter how many sizes she would make the poor salesgirl bring her. Funny!

Glued to the expensive luggage display and lost in wanderlust is an example of the most versatile body type, the willowy *banana*. Too bad her sloping shoulders are covered under a cheap T-shirt. The only cut that works for her is a low décolleté that shows off the long neck flowing into gracefully bent shoulders. But, the straight shoulders of her shirt move like they have a life of their own.

This one, struggling in cheap jeans that conceal her waist and squish her sides is the Hourglass, the most perfect and the rarest body type. Looks terrible in most clothes. Not actually a fruit, but there were so few Hourglasses, that nobody cared about this exception to the fruit classification system.

If only women bothered take a few weeks and learn

these basics . . . of course, she might be out of commission if the customers stopped buying heaps of clothes they could not possibly wear, only to return for more because nothing they bought worked.

And Apple Blossom needed her commissions.

Apple Blossom was inspired by dreams of her own design salon, and in her mind, was already spreading wings in the available parts of the mall and hiring her own models. She looked up at the current customer twirling on the stand between the mirrors, trying to surreptitiously read the price tag. She'd make a good model. Tall and willowy, and best of all, she is a classic Banana. Bananas do not look like much once you undress them, but they can look good in ninety percent of the catalogue.

Funny she is stuck on this dress, though. This dress is made for an Hourglass, the shape that looks best naked but is all but impossible to dress. Unless, of course, you go through the trouble of building a dress specifically for an Hourglass. In that case, Wow!

This customer could pull off just about everything else in the store, but she is stuck on the only thing on the floor that absolutely does not suit her. Apple Blossom considered the metaphoric significance of the moment, but the Banana interrupted with a question.

"What do you think?" The Banana twisted herself around like a dog trying to catch a tick on her butt.

"I wonder if Alterations could help," thought Apple Blossom. Lariska, the émigré Alterations gal from Tomsk was a true wizard. On wool jersey, she could cut out the middle of the hem, knit together the top and bottom parts, and—

"Vuala, ze shape intakt!" Lariska would declare triumphantly.

She could shorten the sleeves without disturbing the shape of the cuff and the line of darts. Or make the jacket fit to freakishly narrow shoulders of an important Chinese client. If anybody could make an hourglass dress fit a Banana, that'd be Lariska. But the entire Alterations department was out for a wedding. Plus, one had to admit: it'd be a shame to cut this dress, almost like defacing a Rembrandt masterpiece.

Impossible choice!

"How do I look?" the Banana inquired, a little more insistently this time.

Apple Blossom briefly wondered if she should treat this as an alteration emergency. She had Lariska's number in her cell phone and could cajole her into coming in. But then, there were considerations: Lariska had to be handled with care. There were some alterations that could not be done, and in those times, Lariska was a liability. They once lost fifty thousand worth of business because Lariska blurted out right to the customer who was trying on a beautiful pant suit jacket:

"Take off! Take off now! Such specially straight shoulder on your sloppy shoulder. You see? Is stupid. Is like you grow wing! Take off."

Good chance Lariska's famously blunt ways would sabotage the sale here too:

"Take off aRR-glass. You not aRR-glass. You banan! What? You can not look? You banan!"

Apple Blossom did not have to check the price-tag to know her commission. At ten thousand dollars, The Dress would pay for this quarter's tuition *and* finance her first design. And she'd probably be able to successfully push for the accessories too. The Dress needed the right shoes, and not the kind this Banana was wearing.

Apple Blossom closed her eyes and imagined all the future women she would make beautiful and happy by outfitting them in her own designs. With relief, Apple Blossom saw with great clarity that, in this present instance, self-interest and the moral high ground both counseled that one Banana could be sacrificed in the interest of the Greater Good. *Can't make a salad without cutting a banana,* she decided.

She swallowed, and told the truth:

"This Dress looks very solid. *Very* solid."

Solid was a given. It was the season's height of fashion—*cool wool*, lightweight Merino wool, each thread three times finer than a human hair, diluted with a thread of silk. It was cut by the best British tailors.

"Would you like me to save it for you?" pressed Apple Blossom gently.

The Floozy sensed deceit. That sly look in the salesgirl's eye. Like the girl knew something about her, some secret that Floozy herself didn't know. The Floozy had seen that look before. Heck, she'd given that look. That's how one looked at those uppity wives who hadn't the faintest clue that somebody was sleeping with their husbands.

"No way," decided Floozy, "It's insane to worry. That stupid round cow is just jealous."

As far as Floozy was concerned, The Dress was it. It had been love at first sight.

The Mistress had chosen her court armor. Sensible, and solid, and expensive, and yet somehow very, very feminine and familiar. It was like she had worn this dress before, in another life. Like it was her lucky dress once somewhere back in her past.

THE JUDGE

"WHY ON EARTH is she wearing this?" hissed The Raccoon, not known for his subtlety, "Is this a joke?"

The Floozy's figure that could bend to its marvelous Banana shape almost any textile found from Target to Belk, had finally met its match. The soft, lightweight, cool wool affair with silky stitching and hundreds of man-hours dedicated to drafting the patterns was a tailoring masterpiece that aimed to cherish, celebrate and enhance every feminine curve of the shapely body type for whose contours it was designed. Before the wool was cut, the patterns were drawn and redrawn on sleek paper, then tested on a cheaper fabric—cut and sewn, draped over dressmaker's dummies, critiqued, adjusted, redrawn again, remade into another test fabric dress, until, finally, the pattern was perfect. The crafty use of darts, plain, French and curved, molded the soft fabric to the shape of the perfect female form.

The contour of the breasts was underscored with deep French darts; the hourglass shape of the model's thin waste and ample bottom was strikingly set with double-pointed darts. Each cut and seam and fold was placed exactly where needed with the precision of the engineering of a spacecraft. A mistake in five millimeters would have produced a disaster. Only then, the precious fabric was brought in, and the precise contours of the pattern were drawn in tailor chalk, then stitched over in long white marking thread, and finally there came the time of Gargantuan scissors.

All said and done, the Dress was a sonnet to the female shape, and not just any female shape—to the real deal, the Hourglass with identical hips and bust matching each other at 36 inches exactly, separated by the drop of 24-inch waist, and topped with straight shoulders. The classic Hourglass. Most feminine of all body types, and also the one most difficult for the tailor, a shape often lost in ill-fitting clothes. But The Dress was cut from perfect fabric for the perfect female body. The

Dress knew it, and would not lightly brook any variances from perfection.

And herein brewed the problem.

As The Floozy made her entrance, and her high-heeled foot touched the courtroom floor, the Perfect Dress separated itself from The Floozy's right buttock, and formed an air-filled balloon, gently billowing just below The Floozy's waistline. Apparently catching the drift, the owner of The Dress gripped the fabric just beneath her butt cheek and gave a short, stealthy yank aimed to adjust the air balloon into submission. This defensive action initially appeared to help. The Dress was in shock for a few seconds, but then bounced back and spread an air pocket around the small of the back, where it knew The Floozy could not see it. That maneuver a success, The Dress mischievously inflated another air bubble just above The Floozy's modestly endowed rack.

"Is she patting her breasts?" whispered The Raccoon, never the one to be a gentleman in the face of the opposition's little embarrassments.

The Floozy was mumbling to herself. We could not hear the words, but we were pretty sure she was telling off The Dress:

"You behave yourself now. This is a serious day, a very important day."

The Dress sprouted another air pocket, lifting its

shoulder all the way toward The Floozy's ear, as if it wanted to whisper, "Darling, I'm confused by your body and we are in real trouble."

And there was, indeed, trouble.

The Dress had clear and detailed instructions from its exacting British tailors:

"I'm flowing down your back," The Dress narrated its credo, "I'm barely splashing over your waist in a waterfall . . . perhaps just one splash touches your waist, so the men in the room would notice . . . and I slide on, spilling up your bottom, tightly up the half-curve, but just before the fabric spills down, I linger so there's *almost* enough time for men in the room to go 'Oh' . . . But before they exhale, you step forward, *my dear*, and I run to the front . . . Down your right breast, I fall in a concave waterfall of cool wool, cascade barely a whisper above your waist, gently falling over the curve of your front thigh . . ."

"That's sweet," muttered back Floozy, "but what's the problem? Why aren't you concave cascading?"

"I'm in trouble," whispered back The Dress.

"What is it?" Floozy raised her muttering to an impatient grumble and pinched The Dress on the waist.

"I am stuck," whispered back The Dress. "I'm stuck on your waist. It's too thick."

"What did you just say about my waist?" threatened The Floozy.

———

"Stand for the Judge," barked the bailiff, arriving out of nowhere, "Honorable John Dawning presiding!"

"Sit, sit," energetically contradicted His Honor "Judge Shorty," an unimaginatively nick-named young fellow that stood no more than 5'4" short. Judge Shorty entered unadorned by any judicial regalia and lacked the arthritic infirmity which the general population so firmly associates with judicial solemnity. But he made the vertical leap up to the judicial bench with the unmistakable familiarity of the owner. What Shorty may have lacked in height, he compensated by good posture, speed and solid muscle. He liked his constituency to know that. A robe obscured the muscular display and, therefore, was only worn when absolutely necessary. Also, he considered sneaking up on the lawyers to be jolly good fun, and there's not much sneaking can be done in a robe.

We all scrambled to jump up.

"Be at ease," insisted Shorty, rummaging on his secretary's desk.

Nobody eased up. We stood at attention anyway, in hopes that the party with the most obsequious posture would get a few extra points in the discretionary part of the ruling. You never know what might work in court.

Except for Mrs. Grimm. Obsequious was not part of her body vocabulary.

Mrs. Grimm lifted herself up with the easy grace of a lady deciding to powder her nose between meal courses, too refined to stand abruptly and cause her male company to scramble to their feet. This was familiar territory for Mrs. Grimm,—her life was filled with men who stood up when she stood up, and men who had to open car doors when she arrived. She was a warm, caring creature, and she learned to pause before moving, to give them a beat. She was always at ease, never in a hurry.

"Pre-trial motions anybody?" Shorty kept rummaging on the desk, and I paused: better to wait silently and get the judge's full attention. My first tactical error of the day: Floozy's lawyer was already ramping up before the sibilant "s?" in the Judge's "motions?" dissipated in the air.

Opposing counsel did not even start at the beginning of his own sentence:

". . . dismiss because unconstitutional! This law . . ."

"What??" Shorty dropped his rummaging.

The word "constitution" hits any judge right smack on the nose,—it's like vampires confronted by the smell of garlic or the mere shadow of a crucifix. It is an appellate review threat thing.

"What did you say?" Shorty was standing up straight, stretched to the full height of his five foot four on top of the six-foot bench, elbows perked away in a Superman's pose.

Now we had the judge's full attention.

"Bad law," Floozy's lawyer asserted as he mirrored the Superman pose. "Alienation of affections is . . . It ought to be . . . It should . . . Your Honor, be repealed. This here is an opportunity and a challenge. We here must make a stance. Here and now."

We? Way to include the judge in his camp, I thought bitterly, and plunged into the fight:

"Judge, with respect, Your Honor, you can't repeal a law. All due respect, Your Honor's mandate does not stretch that far. That's up to the Legislature. If Mr. Grimm wants a law repealed, he should contact his representative in the Legislature."

"Anything else?" Shorty looked slighted by my attack on the limits of his power and turned away to the opposition, who perked up in the reflected light of judicial grace, and tried to exchange smiles with the judge. But Shorty was in no mood: "You got two minutes, counsel. What's your Constitutional challenge?"

My opposition jumped in mid-sentence like a tape taken off pause: ". . . because the law's a relic. Our society is better than that now. Husbands do not own their wives. We do not let husbands use the horse whip and rape their wives anymore, like they could in the old times, and we should not objectify women's affections either."

"You got a *Constitutional* challenge?" Shorty shifted his standard-issue Aeron chair and tried to shield behind it. The chair was mostly holes and air, and would provide little protection from whatever looming appellate scrutiny might now lurk in the courtroom. "What part of the Constitution are you invoking?"

"The Nineteenth Amendment, Your Honor," The Opposition stepped around his desk and gesticulated patriotically. "That's a clear 19th Amendment violation. Alienation of affection treats women as property. Chattel, Your Honor! Affections are not chattel. Women are not chattel. This alienation law is a hellacious relic. It's misogynistic, and it should be abolished."

"Judge," I interrupted in violation of three separate rules of courtroom decorum, "How does all that apply to *Mister* . . ."

But the Opposition rolled over my orating effort like a steamroller:

"Alienation of Affectionsss!" he hissed his "s"s and spat his "t"s with the gusto of a two year old spitting two cheekfuls of hot porridge in his nanny's face "As a feminist, I personally oppose this anachronistic law, and

I am sure Your Honor, as a feminist . . ." he froze, stopped by the judicial palm commanding silence, and at that precise moment I ramped up to a shout. In the sudden silence of the courtroom, I yelped:

"Mr. Grimm is a *man*. The affections wrongfully alienated are those of a *man*, not a woman, Your Honor. May the Court take judicial notice, please . . . That Mr. Grimm's a *he!*"

"The Court noticed," Shorty did not crack a smile. "I warned you not to interrupt, Ms. Porter, did I not?"

"Eh . . .," I responded sheepishly, because there was no good way to answer this.

"Once more and you're in direct contempt!" announced Shorty. "Direct contempt" is judge lingo which pretty much means dissing a judge to his face. It's punishable by fines and days in jail.

Behind me, Hoppy plopped the box which held our bail money. In case of contempt.

My team's confidence is just overwhelming, I thought.

"You know what," decided Judge Shorty, finally finding the piece of paper that was the subject of his excavation, "I'll see you, counsel, in chambers."

I dislike chambers chats, and so should any lawyer unless he's got connections. Things get said in divorce court chambers. Threats get made. Lawyers get wedged into very uncomfortable positions in chambers. And there's no record of what went on. No witnesses. And no recourse to a higher court.

It's a mousetrap, and that's what we called it.

"Could my assistant . . .," I started.

"Counsel only," threatened Judge Shorty.

The Raccoon shrugged with the hatred of an innocent, put-upon victim of hierarchical bigotry—undeservedly dubbed a second-class citizen *again*—but sulkily stayed behind.

I filed out, following Shorty and Floozy's lawyer. Behind me, The Raccoon grumbled "I'll see you, counsel, in the *mousetrap*," in perfect imitation of the Judge's pitch. In the moment, I did not think it funny.

THE MOUSETRAPS

"MOUSETRAPS" WERE THE closet-sized cubby-holes just off the courtroom exit, which served as make-shift offices to whichever judges happened to preside over the courtrooms that day. The actual chambers were located five floors up—clean and airy suites of rooms, as seen on TV. But Shorty's command "in chambers" did not get us up to the ninth floor. Ninth was a sacred place where trial lawyers were seldom invited. Ninth floor chambers were for committee meetings and an occasional pow-wow to settle an appellate record. Our matter was not nearly elevated enough to warrant the dignity of the Ninth.

"Mousetraps" were plunked around the corridor at a rate of one cubbyhole per every two courtrooms. Two judges sometimes had to share. They were popular destinations for a quick discovery meeting with the lawyers, a meet to get the agreed-on orders signed, or a for a place where judges could lean on lawyers without the clients present, all off the record. Also, that's where the judges kept their dirty coffee cups, half-eaten snacks and their street coats.

Without stepping into the mousetrap, Shorty hooked his arm inside, and, after three nervous jerks, liberated his polyester robe off the hook.

"You can wait here," grunted Judge Shorty, moving away from the entrance and showing us in.

In lieu of a window, the wall was brightened by a two feet by two square spot of fire-engine red—a photo of the actual fire engine, which served the background of the "Firefighters for Rescue Dogs"-themed calendar. April was portrayed by a *female* firefighter, caught on camera in a wife-beater shirt, her tan naked biceps wrapped skillfully around a "just saved" liver-colored puppy with blue wistful eyes. April's own eyes were the exact same color as the dog's, but enhanced by just the right amount of eyeliner.

"For charity," offered my opposition, noticing the direction of my gaze. I reckoned April was an especially well-endowed month for charity, because we were now in August.

"Sit tight. Wait here, I'll just be a minute," repeated Judge Shorty, trotting away while donning his judicial robe.

The door of the adjacent courtroom let in a buzz of stressed voices, and then swallowed the judge as it closed behind him with a soft clunk.

"DV court," sighed Floozy's lawyer, abruptly losing his war spirit and addressing no one in particular. Domestic Violence courts are specialized courts designed to provide victims with enhanced safety and a sense of security.

Because of a well-publicized spat with the Chief District Court Judge, Shorty's courtroom schedule was so intense that it'd make the lunchtime rush at Dizengoff's look blissfully unhurried by comparison. Today, Judge Shorty was running two courtrooms at once—and it was a light day for him, too, since our courtroom only had the one case. The DV court, however, was packed so tight that the standing places were pressing elbows into each other and, if one needed to liberate papers from an inside pocket, that necessitated a struggle with the neighbor's side. On the lawyers' side of the courtroom, the jockeying for supremacy in line was escalating beyond cranky to palpably angry. On the *pro se* side benches to which lawyerless parties were relegated, the bailiff had to confiscate two cell-phones, threaten a shrill middle-aged man, and was now controlling the room by the sheer intimidating power of his piercing gaze. It was high time for the courtroom to finally be graced with a judge. The Chief District Court Judge would be hearing a report of Shorty's "inefficiency" any time now. Somebody in the DV courtroom would surely squeal to high heaven. Well, at least to the Chief Judge, who was here the closest earthly semblance of the power of high heaven.

"Pissed off the Chief," my opposition observed, adding fresh grist to the rumor mill as he prepped for a patch of mental hibernation, his one sharp knee balanced on the other.

Like drug dealers, judges always make you wait. For a lawyer, it takes skill and savvy to contain the nervous energy of the motion morning and just idle in wait. But it's a must. If you don't idle your engines, you'll be a complete wreck and a babbling idiot by the time, hours later, when your three precious minutes with the Judge finally do arrive.

Checking out mentally is a trick that helps. It also

helps to rejoice that you are being paid to wait.

I wondered if my opposition was also charging by the hour. Or at least if he was *promised* payment by the hour. The Floozy herself likely had nothing, but her interests were backed up by *Mr. Grimm.*

Surely?

I almost asked, but thought better of it and stuck to the safe topics instead:

"What did Shorty do to the Chief?"

Apparently, I hit gold: "You don't know?"

I shook my head *"I'm new here,"* but no encouragement was necessary: The Story of Shorty was already bubbling out of my new buddy like warm sparkling water from a shaken bottle. As it turned out, Shorty was a local celebrity, and it was not often that a Ducklingburg native could find fresh ears for that piece of town lore. The story was told so many times around town that even the accompanying hand gestures were perfected.

Anybody passing our mousetrap would see two lawyers deeply engrossed in the fascinating story of Shorty's life and election.

Judge Shorty was stuck in his own mousetrap.

When his non-lawyer friends asked, he'd say that the cheese was his elusive dream of leisure, supported by a hefty State pension. Ninety-six thousand dollars a year from his grateful constituents, every year, until the day a judge dies. That was the dream, he'd say. And—he'd have health coverage for the entire family—useful when the kids would come. And—so long as he was a judge, he'd never have to buy malpractice insurance. Shorty came to despise the humiliating annual malpractice insurance review back when he was a private practice lawyer: the protracted inquisition into all his faults, real or imaginary, the endless paperwork themed "steps done to prevent past problems from re-occurring," topped by the five-thousand-dollar invoice from a reluctant C-rated carrier. Avoiding the humiliation of the annual review process was why he ran for election as a judge in the first place. Or that's what he told his buddies, anyway.

Yes, like many other American states, South Duck's judges were elected, every four years, on the same ballot as every other common politician. Shorty despised politicians, and ran a very different campaign. He threw his name in on whim, without asking for support from the local lawyers' Bar, or the local judges, or whatever behind-the-scenes forces that ultimately get to decide the elections. There was no point in asking for their support: he was not going to get a nod from the lawyers.

Shorty was a newbie lawyer at the time: he had no "leadership experience," no "party endorsements," and no "platform"—whatever all those words meant. Considered as a lawyer, he was "nobody." Frankly, the two "prominent Ducklingburg lawyers" who competed for the same judicial seat barely paid any mind to Shorty's entrance into the race—that is, until they saw his *full* name on the yard signs: John "Shorty Vertical Leap" Dawning, and realized that he was *that* John Dawning—the now retired shortest point guard player in South Duck basketball history—five foot four inches. With a 40-inch vertical leap. The fans would not forget a player like that. Shorty may have lacked the "leadership and platform," but he had what no other lawyer in town could get: instant name recognition and in-state hero status.

The morning after Ducklingburg Bar put two and two together, all three local rags ran a three page spread of "judicial candidates analysis." They praised the experience of the incumbent judge and illustrated his success with colorful graphs. They remarked with approbation of the initial challenger's "vision" and "prominence." The only mention of Shorty was his name, accompanied by a dry "also running for the seat." But that was enough—his name. When it came time for the popular vote, the Ducklingburgers did not care a dead fly for the papers' view of judicial capabilities of the boring lawyers. Who could tell those weaselly bastards apart, anyway? What the good people of Ducklingburg did care about, however, was sports. When they saw Shorty's name on the ballot, their natural inclination was to circle it and to cross off all competition. Shorty won his first popular election 97% to 3%, and never looked back.

Would it surprise you to learn that most of the local lawyers and judges—including Shorty's boss, the Chief Judge—sneered at Short's election as an affront to the sacred standards of the South Duck judiciary? No, of course you wouldn't be surprised!

———————

Staying on the bench may be a mousetrap, but at least it had some attractive cheese. It was true that the dream pension would not start paying for at least another quarter century, and would only vest if a he could remain on the judicial bench for six more years. (Ten years altogether was required. Shorty had done four years, and holding on to his bench and gavel was about as easy as riding a wild bull.) Judgeship was a never-ending series of battles, all waged with one eye on the ever-critical Court of Appeals and the other on his boss here in the Ducklingburg Court. Shorty was exhausted. And he was not sure he was winning the battle to endure.

The morning that he wearily took his bench to hear Grimm v. Grimm was one of those career-killing mornings when the feeling of defeat hovered palpably in the air. Judge Shorty could feel the force dragging him down to once again hit the pavement of private practice. His livelihood was headed swiftly into the crapper and, worst of all, he did not know what exactly was pushing him down. It was not something in particular that he could identify.

Returning to private practice was Shorty's worst nightmare. He'd have to start at the bottom again— jostling for cases, making monthly payments for the blinking ever-jamming copier, trying to collect overdue bills from deadbeat clients.

He'd be guilty of borrowing somebody else's Westlaw legal search account in order to split the online fees—a common divorce practitioners' trick—the lawyer's equivalent of stealing a neighbor's cable service. He'd done it before and would have to do it again. This shit guarantees a State Bar inquisition if you are caught. Shorty still had shivers when he thought about it.

What if his not-so-trusted friends and co-conspirators would rat him out? Would he deny he'd done it?

In State Bar investigations, the worst of all the

punishments comes for having the cheekiness to lie to State Bar Investigators. In his bravest moments, Shorty told himself that he'd just be blunt if the State Bar investigators showed up at his door: "Look, everybody steals Westlaw subscriptions. You should lean on these fat cats at Westlaw to make their service affordable."

After the first four years as a judge, he was pretty sure he'd never make it in the wild again. He was already too invested in the dream symbolized by his judicial robes. He would not admit it to friends, but the pension was not his only dream. He aimed higher. And he certainly did not want to fall down. Private practice . . . That would entail meeting the lawyers who used to literally look up at him, on equal footing. He thought of the humiliation.

The other lawyers . . . they will still call me Judge for a few months and speak in hushed tone, then the "Judge" title will sound in mockery, and they'll switch to "former Judge," and pretty soon it'll be "Shorty could you cover me for calendar call in Iredell County, 'cause I can't make the drive, and the Judge there is a raving ass? There's twenty bucks in it for you."

And yes, he knew that the lawyers and his judge colleagues called him "Shorty" out of disrespect. On the other hand, that nickname was a term still applied almost-reverentially by the voters who remembered his basketball heroics for the University of South Duck.

Shorty was smart enough to remember his grandmother's saying that "Sometimes you've gotta take the bitter with the better."

No, he decided, for the millionth time, he'd hold on. And he'd move up. Shorty did not lie when he said he was in it for the pension, but he did not wear his heart on his sleeve either. The *real* dream was to take the Chief Judge's place. That was the real gold. But biding time until the dream retirement vested was a sage first-step option. Only six more years.

THE GAME

THE TRIAL JUDGE of Ducklingburg county must fulfill a trio of requirements: the judge's rulings must be quick, true to the law, and politically correct. Shorty's heartfelt intention was to defend his position on all three of these criteria. If he fell short on even just one, the Chief's retaliation would supply grounds to push him tumbling off the bench, even before the next election. Shorty was determined to fight on until his last drop of blood was shed. But did he have enough blood to last through the constantly bleeding drip-drip-drip?

Optically, speed was Shorty's first order of business and his primary worry. Divorce judges' dockets grow by about fifty cases a day, but nevertheless must move swiftly and smoothly. Unattended cases must not languish or linger in a judge's care. Justice delayed, as they say, is justice denied, whatever that may mean. Orders pronounced in court must be delivered to the parties with all deliberate speed . . . and all that jazz.

In thoughtful consideration of his precarious position, Shorty stepped up his game. What he needed to meet the first prong of good judgeship was more time, to squeeze at least nine courtroom hours out of each day. The Chief Judge would soon come trolling to find a fault with Shorty. The #1 criticism was always the festering pile of unfinished cases. But on that ground, Shorty'd be ready.

He marshalled the prophylactic defense of working through lunch. He chewed his falafel and pickle carryout without ever stepping off the bench, nodding to the lawyers to go on with their arguments, taking elaborate care to wipe off any greasy fingers before he touched the files, and pecking notes on his computer only with a scrupulously clean finger. He even stocked one of his drawers full of baby wipes to clean off the crumbs and the oil spills without missing a bit of lawyers' pontifications. That gave him forty-five extra minutes each day, and he was quite proud of himself for getting ahead. That is, until the Chief District Court Judge got wind of it. The office of the Chief District

Court Judge counter-attacked with a *Memorandum on Judicial Decorum*, in which the Chief District Court Judge condemned certain unnamed judges for their "derogatory and patronizing attitude towards the litigants"—the *gall* of chewing fast food right in the faces "of the loving parents who brought the sacred matter of their children's custody into our fine court."

The Chief's move made squeezing work into the lunch hour impossible, but Shorty was not easily discouraged.

In response to the *Memorandum on Judicial Decorum*, Shorty nixed the falafel and the pickle, but continued to hold bench through lunch, keeping himself nourished with the "BeSlimSwift" drink, which he hid in his Size XXL coffee mug. BeSlimSwift's advertising guaranteed that he'd have "energy lasting for five hours." It did not lie. Unfortunately, it did not tell the entire truth either. The gooey drink also had the undesirable side effect of making the Judicial small intestines feel as though His Honor had swallowed an entire black hole, an unnerving force settling in and sucking on the Judge's innards. But, true to the drink's label, he did not feel hungry. And Shorty was not going to let one little intestinal black hole interfere with his career path. Fueled by the drink—and perhaps also by the adrenaline of his precarious work situation—his productivity went sky high. He disposed with the petty discovery motions, awarded temporary custody, sent deadbeats out to look for work and come back with proof of thirty job applications in thirty days . . . Judge Shorty was on fire!

His system worked splendidly for two days, until one court afternoon when a child support delinquent started grumbling about the shameful inequity: the courtrooms had a "no food or drink" policy.

"The judge's minions get him fresh coffee," grumbled the low-life, "but we here are packed together waiting on His Highness like cattle before slaughter."

The delinquent's plaint sure packed a powerful image. Worried about his reputation for political correctness and equity, Shorty adjusted by liberating the courtroom. The only judge on the floor who allowed beverages in his courtroom, he was the man of the hour. But his joy was short-lived. By the end of the day, the cleaning crew had to be called for an extra shift to deal with soda spills along the benches which lined a courtroom which smelled like a train station, looked like piss, and made shoes stick to the floor.

The bailiff of the day happened to be on Chief's snitching duty and, as a result, the circulating Chief's *Memorandum* swiftly got amended to add a new paragraph on the "Judicial obligation to maintain courtroom decorum *and cleanliness.*"

That night, Shorty swore revenge. He had been

badly out-maneuvered, and he knew that. But, Shorty was no quitter.

He retaliated by skipping *all* food or drink on the bench, worked his courtroom non-stop for the full eight-thirty to five-thirty stretch, and declared victory. Judge Shorty's courtroom moved the swiftest and was the cleanest on the entire family floor. And the next day, when his mailbox was blissfully devoid of any more Chief's Memos, Shorty congratulated himself on clear and definite victory: he found his groove, and would get the "best judge of the year" star. Shorty was jubilant.

Once again, his victory lap was shortsighted. The contest of wills was far from over. Indeed, Shorty and the Chief District Court Judge were barely entering the middle game.

This time, instead of circulating a neutral-sounding memo to every divorce court judge of the County, the Chief District Court Judge took a direct approach: he wrote personally to Shorty. A creased cheap envelope was in Shorty's dedicated mailbox, placed indelicately on top of the usual medley of colorful Continuing Legal Education flyers and thick letters from lawyers arguing viciously about the exact phrasing of pending judicial orders. Anybody passing mailboxes on the Judges' floor could plainly see the envelope, and form the obvious conclusion: bad news. Embarrassing. Shorty's career was quickly headed for a world of hurt and the weasel of a Chief did not even have the decency to deliver his attack in person.

The Chief Judge's office address was printed all-caps in flat black ink on the envelope. Shorty's name was peeping through the plastic window. Even though the Chief's office was in the same flight of suites, and even though both men's mailboxes were in pigeonhole cubes on the same wall, the envelope was meter-stamped, a precaution to mark the day of delivery, figured Shorty. The day was Friday, seventy-two hours before Judge Shorty took his bench to preside over Grimm v. Grimm's jury selection day, then glowered at the file and herded the lawyers into chambers.

THE LETTER

"**CHIEF JUDGE SENT** him a *letter*. Judge Shorty'll not last through the term," gossiped Floozy's lawyer as confidently as he'd talk of this morning's stock prices.

We'd been waiting for half an hour, and had covered the weather and vacations already, the consensus about those vital issues being:

Hot.

None.

"Let's settle the case, Porter," suggested my opposition, concluding evidently that the ice between us was sufficiently melted.

"What's the offer?" I took out my phone to start typing. By their professional code of ethics, lawyers are required to take any offer of settlement and bring it to the client without delay, and in complete detail, however preposterous the offer may be. It's easier for me when offers come in writing—those can just be forwarded. For verbal offers, I do my best to type them out verbatim.

"We need to settle," he repeated almost pleadingly.

"I'm ready. What's the offer?"

Fingers on the phone, I waited. And waited a few seconds longer. No offer was forthcoming. I peered up from the phone screen and stumbled over his stare, looking straight at me with friendly curiosity, the way one inspects unfamiliar but unthreatening animal.

"Why don't *you* make me an offer?" he actually smiled, a reassuring smile, like he was daring me to make an unpleasant but necessary step. A caring guardian would have this look, suggesting to a child: "Why don't you have a nice spoonful of tasty fish-oil now?"

The guy had mad negotiation skills!

"You start," I gripped the phone again.

"You walk away," dictated the Great Negotiator. His hands folded, he waited for me to type it in: "walk away."

"Anything else?" My fingers were still over the

phone screen.

"We don't counter-claim for defamation," he scrunched his shoulders together.

"You might have missed that deadline nine months ago."

"What do you mean? It's not compulsory." The Great Negotiator seemed sincerely confused.

"I said no."

"We won't ask for fees," his left knee started vibrating, and he grasped his shoulders tighter.

I typed obediently. The rules of legal ethics demand that I take the offer to my client. Any offer. Nonsense or not. Even if the offer borders on insult. So my job was to take dictation.

"Done. I'll take it to my client. Who will take instant offense at it. You got any real offers?"

The Great Negotiator cradled his face in both palms, swayed for a moment, then opened his palms, the way actors sometimes do in rehearsals, revealing a change of mood or persona.

"Ten thousand." He was serious and sincere now. "Look. My woman's got nothing. Ten large is the best that she can swing, and I would take a pay cut."

"Sweet of you."

"It's true. You should take it."

"I'll notify my client of the offer, but I will not recommend it."

"My woman has no money," The Great Negotiator had the professional habit of divorce lawyers of referring to clients by gender labels.

Two divorce lawyers working on a settlement would say:

Lawyer 1: My woman needs the alimony check yesterday.

Lawyer 2: Could you tell your woman to wait a week? My man just got fired.

The professional lingo may seem offensive, but it's oddly helpful, the same way it helps to color our property division charts in pink and blue. Alas, same-sex marriages now present a linguistic challenge.

Despite the honestly looking extended palms of my opposition's hands, I was not falling for the "no money" scheme.

"Ask your woman's benefactor," I suggested.

"Who, Mr. Grimm?" the Great Negotiator believably faked surprise, "He ain't got money either. Your woman is the rich one."

"Sure. Whatever you say. Anything else?"

He shook his head, and I closed the phone app and switched my focus to bringing my iPhone's screen back to its original factory shine with the aid of my pant hem.

He did not let up. "Take the ten large. Tell your woman, make sure she knows: I'm shaving my bill. I might even do it for free if it ends this."

"Why would you do that?"

"For my personal belief."

"You believe in something?"

"This alienation of affections suit is a disgrace. It's a shame on the profession. You *will* be sanctioned for filing it."

"By whom?"

Judge Shorty famously had never sanctioned a lawyer. Not that there was anything sanctionable in my filings anyway.

"*His* term is short," maintained the Great Negotiator ominously.

"Even shorter if he listens to your rhetoric. You *want* Shorty to catch a reversal?"

"You are fixing to catch a night in jail for contempt," he ended the pleasantries, "Mind your own problems."

I minded for a minute, and changed the subject back to gossip:

"What was in the Chief Judge's letter, do you know?"

"Not a friendly pat on the back, that's for sure."

———

Shorty had waited to open the Chief Judge's letter

until he'd driven most of the way home. He did not want to risk a secretary or a colleague walking in. On the other hand, waiting all the way until he was home with his wife was also tricky. Daria took his career way too personally. He needed to prepare her for the news.

Shorty pulled up his leased Audi into a Harris Teeter parking lot, which at 5:30 on a Friday was apparently the place to be. He angled for the last parking spot, but missed. A spirited canary yellow motorcycle cut in out of nowhere and made it from 60 to full stop right in front of Shorty's conservative silver bumper. Last thing any judge needed was an embarrassing parking lot fender-bender! He started a reconnaissance loop around the lot, but got stuck behind the huge brown rear of the Ford Transit Wagon that seemed parked. There was no way to see what had stopped the monstrosity, and Shorty gave up on finding the perfect place to read the letter.

The dead stop behind this egregious gas guzzler is as good place as any to say bye-bye to my dreams, Shorty decided.

The entire pile of today's mail was scattered on the passenger seat. Picking out the fateful envelope from the pile, Shorty used a plastic knife to neatly open it and extract the letter:

Dear Judge John Dawning,

It gives me great pleasure to be the first one to congratulate you upon the honor of being selected as our top candidate for the first complex track judge in Middle Duck County. This promotion gives an opportunity . . .

The letter ran for three more paragraphs, pontificating on the advantages of the "complex track judge" designation. Shorty had heard about the program. If he got the job, it definitely would be a step up. His courtroom would be transformed. Instead of holding court over the common herd of defeated deadbeats and doleful lawyer-less mothers of five, squeezing five different but equally unwilling and suspicious fathers for a few hundred bucks, he'd oversee "complex-track cases"—multi-million dollar disputes, intricate questions of cutting-edge law, the most expensive and litigious lawyers and maybe even snatch a few column-inches in the Ducklingburg Gazette.

It was a promotion!

Or, at least, it was a step towards a promotion. And the Chief *congratulated* him.

Fifteen minutes later, he was home, jubilantly calling Daria from the bottom of the stairs. It was Friday, and time to drink Champagne with his wife!

THE JUDGE'S WIFE AND THE LETTER

DARIA DAWNING (née Daria Yurievna Mazurova) graduated with a red diploma—the equivalent of summa cum laude in the U.S.—from the Department of Law at the prestigious Siberian University of Tundra, on the Northern border of Tmutarakan County. The rigorous five-year law school program of Russian Universities included Classic legal philosophy, which was taught in the original Latin and Greek, but also had seminars on "American Law and Economics," where articles by Posner and Goetz were studied in translation. All in all, Daria was a talented and well-rounded lawyer.

None of that was doing her any good in Ducklingburg, where nobody spoke Russian, or Latin, or Greek, or even any French. But, by God, if Daria's dreams of a legal career were gone—or at least indefinitely suspended—the least she could do was live vicariously through her lawyer husband John-chik. John was going to be a bigshot in the world of Law, if she could help it.

Daria's command of Latin and French was a big help with English, but it was only her first year in the country, and her language skills were rough. She could read better than she could speak, she could speak better than she could understand, and, of course, legal contracts and scholarly articles had all the words she already knew, and so were much easier than conversations with the grocer. The grocer understood hardly a word of her French-accented English, and did his best to keep away, lest the grocer's wife might "think something." (Grocer and his wife both assumed that Daria was a catalogue bride.)

While John was at work, Daria went through his ABA Quarterly with a dictionary and highlighter, marking the important parts for her husband.

She looked forward to the days when her spoken English would improve enough to have long dinner talks with her husband, debating fine points of the law and mocking the uninitiated. Just like back at the Uni.

What Daria did not yet know was that in approximately eighteen months, when she would reach her spoken English goal, she would be in for a second shattering disappointment. Living vicariously through her husband's legal career was not going to be an option. Her John-chik emphatically did not have the makings of a scholar.

She heard John calling from downstairs, and understood the words "complex," "litigation," and "The Chief." When she ran to the landing and saw her darling, words were no longer necessary. He was holding his arms up, in the universal victory sign. His left hand was holding a bottle of extremely cheap Champagne (bought at a gas station, but to Daria, foreign and therefore exotic at least until it got uncorked and tasted). But, better yet, in his right hand, John was holding—and waving—a letter. A good letter does not need translation into any language. The implications are universally understood.

She jumped in place, and pretended to slide down the handrail, a precarious practice she brought from Siberia, where multiple levels of clothing muffled any fall.

"No sliding!" he opened his arms as if to catch her fall. And she landed in his arms, softly, a two-point landing.

After the rollercoaster day, Judge Shorty was really hoping for a quiet evening, vegging out with a remote in his hand, slipping into a total mindlessness with his wife curled up beside him.

"Did you do anything interesting today," he asked cautiously. He was really hoping for some comforting small talk. Anything around the house would do. Rosebushes doing better, peaches were on sale, neighbor's spaniels got a trimming. All fascinating topics. But not with Daria.

She was pointing at the promotion letter he left lying on the kitchen table. Of course, she'd want to scrutinize the thing.

"I am wonder," she started politely, "I shall have read letter? Is possible?"

Daria had a preference for participles and gerunds, regardless of what she tried to say.

"You want to read the letter?" he corrected.

"Thank," she was always happy when he took the trouble to correct her English.

She uncurled from his side and dashed into the kitchen, reappearing with a highlighter, sharpened pencil and an English-French dictionary. Shorty did not have an English-Russian dictionary among his books, but it did not seem to hinder her.

"Here you go," he said redundantly. The letter was already in her eager hands.

She stretched out on the rug, on her stomach, propping herself up on her elbows. Gnawing on the highlighter, flipping the dictionary, and kicking her butt with her heels—left, right, left, left, right—she was the picture of contentment.

For a few minutes, Shorty admired the view, then tried to catch her left ankle.

"No meddle youself."

Clearly, there was to be nothing doing until she finished reading.

"If I can't beat it, I'll join you," he propped himself on the carpet next to her, hovering over her shoulder in order to read the paragraph which she was rapidly beading with tiny French translations.

Kindly note that the distinction of the complex track assignment does not immediately relieve the honored judge from completing the judge's existing caseload. As such, a period of adjustment is expected.

"Vot meant '*not . . . relieve*'," she pressed a well-bitten nail into the line.

"Well, it means that I still finish all my old cases. Even though I also get new complex cases."

"Shall listen new, *complex*? And old, easy?"

He nodded.

"And old and new?"

"Yes, I think so. I am not relieved from . . ."

"*Kak* . . . How you do so?"

"What do you mean?"

"Easy old cases? Can listen on evening?"

"No, Daria, there's no night court. I can't hear cases at night."

"New complex cases can listen on evening?"

"Daria, what are you talking about?"

She pushed her finger deep into the letter.

"*Kak* . . . How possible listen *dva* . . . two cases? And old and new? You may split you? Know how?"

"No, Daria, nobody can be in two places at once." He was getting concerned that she was onto something.

"John-chik," she was sitting upright, legs interlaced around ankles, her eyes glinting.

"John-chik, Bad Chief not do *une promotion*," she pronounced promotion "pro-moh-seeyohn," the way the French say it.

"Promotion," he corrected mechanically.

"Thank. Bad Chief—he make you fork."

"Fork? You mean fuck?"

She shook her head impatiently. "No fuck. Fork. Fork is chess. Read."

She dashed to his laptop and typed furiously for a

few seconds, "Read!"

The screen was opened to "chess terms." He read obediently:

Fork [chess] A tactic where a single piece makes two direct attacks.

"John-chik, Bad Chief do fork. You not can do hard cases. You not can do easy cases. You not time. Chief must you split. Not time. Understand?"

He understood. It was a Machiavellian plan, indeed. He'd stepped into an impossible assignment—two caseloads scheduled in the same timeslot.

"It fork," she repeated pensively.

"It *is* a fork."

"Thank."

"What do I do, Daria?"

She did not alter her pose or tone, "Ve fight, of course."

THE GREAT NEGOTIATOR

FLOOZY'S LAWYER WAS an excellent negotiator. He tricked, he bluffed, he bullied, he double-crossed, he flattered. In short, he *negotiated*.

Considered strictly as a trial lawyer, the Great Negotiator left a lot to be desired. His education was sub-par; he did not bother catching up with the daily developments in the law and was, therefore, known to obliviously cite an opinion, three years after it had been overruled. His client service was not good either: he did not always return his clients' phone calls right away, and when he did, there was not much he said that would be of use. He was underqualified, always unprepared and too lazy to care. But when it came to negotiations, his talent sparkled like a freshly polished cubic zirconium. He could make just about every lawyer question his footing. Where his opposition researched, prepared, questioned, re-drafted, hesitated and considered their cases from every angle, The Negotiator never faltered. In his own mind, his case was always the winner— whatever the law or the facts. He did not really bother much looking at the law or the facts, to be honest. Some said that he bluffed, which, I suppose, is true—except that his bluffing was based on honest faith that he had the best hand in the house.

Despite his daftness, laziness and lack of skill, The Great Negotiator got jobs because he dominated the opposition and delivered Results. With a capital "R."

His approach in Grimm v. Grimm was inspired, as usual.

After striking out in the first round, he attempted to start fresh by establishing the alliances: "I like my client. She may be lost a little but she is a nice person."

"She got lost and wandered into my client's bedroom and then got lost and slept with my client's husband?" I returned, predictably.

"You are not drinking your woman's Kool-Aid, are you?" The Negotiator gave me a soulful look of disbelief. "That marriage's dead."

"Take this up with a jury, mate."

"I don't like your woman," he shifted out of his seat and mined his inside pockets for a few seconds. "Gum?"

I shook my head. The olive branch approach was not going to work for him either, not even if he escalated from gum to M&Ms.

The Great Negotiator did not give in. "You won't win, Portia. The good people of South Duck have refused to give money to whiny ex-spouses for the last twenty-five years."

As usual, he was wrong on the law and the facts.

"The good people of our State have not refused to nail the homewreckers. Nobody has asked them in twenty-five years. Now I'm asking. They might well echo our North Carolina neighbors. Nine million? Thirty million?"

"No matter. Even if you hoodwink the jury, I'll tie it up in appeals."

"You've never appealed a thing. You don't know how. You don't even know how to spell *certiorari*."

"And even if you won," The Great Negotiator affably ignored the insult, "my woman has no money. And Mr. Grimm can't give her any."

"You've said that once already."

"You do not want to go to trial, Portia."

"I do."

"Trust me, there is no pot of gold." His smile was disarming. "Don't you believe me?"

"I do," I said truthfully.

Truth is, I believe just about everybody. Not in the sense that I am lacking in intellectual skepticism, I am a lawyer for crying out loud. However, I almost totally lack the ability to distinguish deception from honest statements.

Some people are born naturally skilled at deception recognition; some people acquire the skill though training; and some are neither. Some people just never can tell. I fall into the last category—the ones that never learn. The non-verbal clues, body tics, the micro—and other expressions—are lost on me. I had tried to combat this vocational defect by learning from the experts—books written by former FBI agents with clever titles like "What Every Body Is Saying," or "Advanced Interviewing Techniques" which promised to teach me to recognize what people were secretly thinking. I tried video courses cleverly titled "Do You Know When Someone is Lying to You?" Some of these courses were supposedly made especially for lawyers—those turned out to be particularly useless. I talked to jury consultants. I bought all three seasons of "Lie to me," and watched them thrice.

Supposedly, the truth is written all over people's faces. I don't see it. Frankly, I am not sure that people who claim to see it aren't charlatans.

"You ought to trust me," repeated The Negotiator

with pleading sincerity, "Mr. Grimm's not putting up any money here. Ten large is the best you'll get. Why don't you trust me?"

"I do, you have an honest face."

"You will recommend my offer, then?"

"Sorry."

"I don't understand. You said you trust me."

"I trust everybody," I explained truthfully. "So I trust nobody."

"Huh? I don't get it."

"If your food smells rotten, you are not going to eat it, right?"

He half-shook his head.

"Smells bad, so you know not to eat it?"

He spat out his gum, and stared quizzically.

"Now suppose everything smelled fine to you, all the time. Could you rely on sniffing your food? No, I don't think so, you'd end up dead pretty quickly!"

"I . . . So what are you saying, Portia?"

"That I can't smell it when you are lying."

"What does that mean?"

"Means I won't dare to eat it."

The Great Negotiator was flummoxed. He met his match: a mark he could neither flatter nor con because I was too daft to even play, and I knew it. There was nothing else to say about Grimm vs. Grimm. The only thing left was small talk.

The Negotiator started first: "What do you think we are doing here?"

We'd been waiting for two hours and a half. And so was the bailiff.

"Suppose the judge forgot he left us here?"

My mind always leaps to ending up in the wrong place.

"Don't be neurotic. It's part of a judge's strategy. It's a tactical solution to force settlement," assured The Negotiator self-servingly. "Trus . . . never mind."

The tactical solution in question, of course, belonged to Judge's wife Daria. The plan was disarmingly simple:

"Hide ze lawyerz. Bad Chief not find. No lawyerz—no problem."

She drew a picture to help him understand his predicament—and the solution. Shorty's predicament was simple: the *impossible* schedule. He could not preside over two courtrooms at once, or as Daria had put it, "you can't double you, no?"

Shorty's physical limitation opened him immediately to criticism from the Chief Judge for "neglecting a working courtroom,"—a big no-no for a judge. The Chief Judge would fight Shorty with a powerful visual—a busy courtroom where everybody— lawyers, clients, witnesses, the bailiff are waiting. And no sign of the judge, nothing in the empty chair up top. A horrible, horrible visual. That would be a career- ending blunder. Something had to be done about it.

"Hide lawyerz." That was brilliantly simple. If there were no lawyers in the courtroom, there was no need for a judge. But how?

"Hide lawyerz *here*," instructed Daria, drawing a disturbingly accurate floorplan of Shorty's courtroom and the surrounding facilities. Daria had insisted on a tour of the courthouse mid-way through their third date—and when he complied, she did not rest until every courtroom Judge John-chick had ever used was thoroughly examined. At the time, Judge John-chick assumed that the escapade into the empty courthouse was her way of flirting: a chase around the courthouse marble did seem oddly romantic. That was an easy mistake on his part: Ducklingburg girls are trained to fake interest in their man's work until the very day he says "I do." But Daria was not faking an interest in his work, in that he was quite sure now. In fact, he grew to wonder if his work was not the only thing that interested her.

"Where Complex Courtroom, here?" Daria interrupted his musings.

He pointed to the square adjacent to his regular courtroom and watched her eyes light up: the architecture yielded to her plan.

"Grimm lawerz wait here," she marked the mousetrap with an elegant checkmark. "Judge John-chik is here," she marked the courtroom next door, where Shorty was scheduled to hear a horde of fifty-three Domestic Violence cases.

Shorty's DV courtroom would be swarming with sizzling bodies and demanded attention. But Grimm vs. Grimm only had the two lawyers. "Grimm lawyerz, let wait," Daria tapped the checkmark on her diagram.

She was right! All any casual observer would see were two lawyers talking—a sacrosanct negotiation scene which would not be disturbed. The clients would not complain, however long they'd wait, and who knows—"zey sit two hourz, zey settle? Maybe?"

Shorty nodded slowly, and Daria said out loud what he was thinking: "Ve not want appeal. No not, yes?"

Reversals by critical Court of Appeals opinions are poisonous to a trial court judge's reputation. Shorty's appellate scorecard was already rather embarrassing, and it seemed about to get a notch worse.

The trial in the Grimm case had not been on Shorty's calendar until two days before—a detail unknown to Mr. and Mrs. Grimm and their lawyers, who would not be told which judge they "drew" until late Friday, right before the week of trial. This reticence about making assignments public was the court's custom. However, on the judges' floor, where the assignments of judges to cases were known weeks in advance, the assignments were avidly discussed and interpreted as tokens of the cachet of a particular judge. Shorty knew his calendar three weeks in advance. The Grimms were a last minute and unwelcome addition. To call the Grimm case undesirable for a trial judge would be charitable. Somebody would for sure appeal, and no matter how he ruled, there was no way to look good on appeal because appellate courts always found some nit to pick. There was simply no way to avoid reputational damage.

Although the law of alienation of affections had been on the South Duck books since the day that the State first *had* its books, the law was far from settled. What's worse, like all of the heart-balm laws, alienation of affections was the favorite shooting target of at least seven different but equally militant and exceptionally active feminist groups. The law, they postulated, was demeaning to women.

Worse still, this sort of politically charged case attracted constitutional challenge like a black suit attracts white cat hair. Which meant that Shorty's rulings about the Grimm case could get appealed all the way to the South Duck Supreme Court, no matter *what* he decided.

Any appeal at all is bad news for a judge. An appeal with a potential to be flung all the way to D.C. and to get splashed in national newspapers is worse. Even potentially ruinous in Shorty's particular predicament. And, considering the law and the players, he'd be appealed whichever way he ruled. Returning to check on the lawyers for the Grimms, his step had a resolute air of a man who must conquer or die.

THE GOAT AND THE EIGHTEEN WHEELER TRUCK

"EXCUSE THE WAIT," an arriving Judge Shorty leaped toward a perch on the side of his desk, his robe flapping like a rooster's wings. A half-filled coffee mug with the crest of Ducklingburg courthouse executed on the checkered background careened precariously, but moved out of the way avoiding an accident.

"Of co-co-course, no problem," stuttered The Negotiator, slinking out of the Honorable's way.

"Any settlement talks?" Shorty credibly faked nonchalance.

"We had some productive negotiation," lied The

Negotiator.

Judge Shorty's eyes sparkled with ill-concealed enthusiasm: "Were you able to reach a settlement, counsel?"

"Ms. Porter stalls," tattled The Negotiator, watching the judge's reaction attentively.

Still perched on the desk, Shorty yanked at the robe hem that was stuck under him and started shuffling and wiggling until both ends of the robe were liberated.

"Any pre-trial motions?" Shorty was all business now.

"Judge, if we are doing motions, could we be back in the courtroom," I pushed both feet into the floor like a sailor ready to take the wind. The judge was handling us, and I detest being handled in the off-the-record precincts of the mousetraps.

"This is just a preliminary," the judge waved me off.

". . . To exclude Plaintiff's exhibits one through seventy-five," The Negotiator was rattling off and gaining speed.

How is it that this man always manages to start speaking in the middle of the sentence?

"What's the objection to one through 75?" queried Shorty, visibly impressed with The Negotiator's breadth of reach. Seventy-five was a big number of exhibits to take away from the jury's eyes.

"More prejudicial than probative," announced The

Negotiator, "courts of South Duck have excluded this sort of exhibits on numerous occasions."

The first seventy-five exhibits I prepared to show the jury were glossy photos celebrating the love and affection reigning in the Grimms' marriage before The Negotiator's client barged in and rudely destroyed their marital bliss. I was proud of my selection. The photos had romance, quirkiness and the subtle humor of first-rated romantic comedy, guaranteed to sway the jury to the side of the marriage. Also, the photos were strictly necessary. To win in an alienation of affections lawsuit, Mrs. Grimm was required to first prove that the marriage was previously viable. Simply showing that Floozy seduced her husband was not enough. Floozy, of course, would insist that there were no affections to alienate. If Floozy could prove this, she'd escape unscathed.

"The South Duck Court of Appeals affirmed exclusion of prejudicial evidence in just such cases," insisted The Negotiator, reaching into his inside pocket for a wad of papers: "Here, *Goat vs. SpeedyWheeler.*" The Negotiator offered the precedent to Shorty, who waved it away: etiquette required The Negotiator to show me the case first.

I always panic when this happens: a new case I had no idea existed. We spent hours scouring all possible precedent for alienation of affections cases. *Goat vs.*

Speedy was not on my list. I would've remembered *Goat*. It was a thick case, too. And the judge kept talking. I snatched the print-out of the Goat case, steeled my face, and tried to concentrate.

It turned out that Mr. Goat was a redneck with a motorcycle hobby. A dangerous sport. In my opinion, it is always only a matter of time with motorcycles. Speedy Wheeler Company was an eighteen wheeler trucking outfit. Its driver was at the end of his nine-hour stretch and did not expect a competition for a lonely stretch of the road at three-forty in the morning.

When the highway patrol came to the scene of the accident, the first mashed piece of flesh that they found was unquestionably a body part, but they could not quite say exactly what it was until the medical examiner arrived and applied her expertise. The motorcycle was caught and dragged a good half a mile, and Mr. Goat was trapped in a twisted knot, his head scraping the pavement in an unequal contest to determine which was harder. What they found first turned out to be Mr. Goat's *face*. Then many, many other parts of Mr. Goat's body were collected, but never all of them. The exhibit offered for the jury in the resultant wrongful death case was a fish-eye photo, capturing parts of the unfortunate Mr. Goat strewn along the long stretch of the highway. Mr. Goat's lawyer planned to blow up the photo to a poster size, and open his case in front of the poster.

"Ladies and Gentlemen of the jury," was the first line of his opening statement, "believe it or not, what you see on the photo is a man . . . and this—moving the laser pointer slowly across the width of the poster . . . is the man's face." An opening like that was dangerously likely to heat up the jury to a multi-million-dollar verdict, whether the driver of the eighteen wheeler was guilty of negligence or not. That's what lawyers call "inflammatory and prejudicial." With *that* photo blown up to *that size*, the eighteen-wheeler was toast before the first witness was sworn in. The federal judge agreed to give the trucker a fighting chance: the color photo was excluded. A black-and-white in eight by five inches was passed around instead, and . . . *wait! That has nothing to do with my case!*

"Judge," I blurted, speaking over the small talk that had blossomed between Shorty and The Negotiator while I was busy dissecting the *Goat.*

"This *Goat vs. the Eighteen Wheeler* opinion is about a wrongful death case with grievous injuries! The pictures excluded from the jury's eyes were blood and gore and human tissue. All *I* have is tennis whites, Christmas lights and cooking dinners together. The *Goat* case is not on point."

Shorty shook his head dismissively. "I agree with the Defense. Exhibits excluded."

"For what reason?" I exclaimed, amazed.

"The jury would be prejudiced into thinking the Grimms had a happy marriage."

"But they *did* have a happy marriage!" I protested simplemindedly.

"Did not," contradicted The Negotiator.

"Judge, that's a central factual issue to the case."

"And you are welcome to try and prove it, counsel. Your client can testify to that. Put her on."

"That's right," echoed The Negotiator, "and I can have her husband testify the whole marriage thing was an empty sham, and had been for years before my client ever appeared."

It is a trick as old as the Sun and the Moon, and yet it gets me every time. The jury—the poor simpletons with the delusions of grandeur, thinking they are arbiters of truth, finders of fact, deciders of fates—can only see what the judge lets them see. Take away the most basic, the most necessary evidence, and the jury will follow the trap like sheep to the slaughter. Except, of course, it is my client's case that was getting slaughtered. Before it even started.

I protested:

"With respect, Judge, let's not make this into 'he said-she said' competition. The younger jurors surely will wonder why there are no pictures."

"She's worried because my guy is so much more trustworthy," sneered The Negotiator.

Shorty snorted a little laugh.

"Judge, that prejudices Mrs. Grimm. And I renew my objection. This motion should be considered on the record, back in the courtroom." At the very least, I needed a record of this injustice, evidence of the fact that I had not just gone insane and torpedoed my own case by forgetting to show the happy marriage to the jury. In court, I could have objected and later appealed with a transcript to prove my argument. But here in the mousetrap there was no record, there was no use in crying objections, and no hope of having a basis to appeal.

Shorty ignored my outburst: "anything else?"

"Since the pictures are out," The Negotiator pressed his luck, "I ask that there is no mention to the jury of anything *in* the pictures."

"Let me see the pictures?" Shorty requested with outstretched hand.

"They are back in court, Your Honor, can we please join them there?" I tried again to move the party back to the courtroom. I needed an appeal of this injustice!

No such luck.

"Anything R-rated on those pictures?" smiled the judge.

"No, Your Honor. Parties, charities, dinners, Christmas Celebrations."

"What else?"

"Trips abroad, Your Honor."

Shorty was silent for about six seconds, and we stopped breathing.

"It's out. No talk of parties, charities, dinners, or Christmases. Especially Christmases. That might offend somebody."

"And the trips, Your Honor," The Negotiator pressed on.

"That's right, no mention of the trips either."

"But Judge, that's . . ." I could not find an adjective that accurately described Shorty's decision and still could be used to his face.

"That's my ruling," Shorty jumped off the table-top perch and finally had his entire robe hem in grip.

"Judge, we are off the record. You can't rule off the record."

"I'm warning you, counsel," roared Shorty, "one word on prohibited subjects and I will be reporting this as a deliberate . . . flagrant . . . contempt of the judge."

Shorty had resorted to the ultimate judicial blackmail. He torpedoed my case here, behind closed doors. To appeal, I needed an objection in court, but mentioning it in court threatened my license. Shorty had me.

"And Judge, you already found her in contempt today," lied The Negotiator helpfully.

"I'll give you five minutes to talk to your client, Ms.

Porter," demanded Shorty, pushing me towards the courtroom entrance, "and report back to *us*. As a Judge, I like to know that I've tried every possible avenue of peaceful settlement."

"Judge, I've talked to her just two hours ago."

"Do it again. Give it a chance, counsel. *We*'ll wait." Judge was united in the pronoun with The Negotiator now. The two men would stay behind and wait for me to explain to the client how I lost the case before it even started.

The Negotiator snickered inappropriately, and I was back in the courtroom, on a mission to see if the settlement landscape had somehow changed since we had left our clients waiting there.

THE DRESS

THE FLOOZY WAS standing alone, obviously ill at ease. Her lawyer had disappeared behind the forbidden door, passible for card-carrying divorce vultures only. Floozy twisted around to make sure that her lover was still there, still had her back, but the rear rows were now empty.

The courtroom air was making her antsy. She started outside for a brief walk around, but at her first step, her attire started griping again:

"I can't flow through," whined The Dress, "I was supposed to flow, but I choked and missed the moment."

"Just move on with it."

"There's nowhere to move," insisted The Dress, "I'm designed to move with the curve, and . . . I'm awfully sorry, but I cannot find the curve. You don't seem to have any."

"Just keep moving."

"There's no curve, and no waist," gasped The Dress.

It tried to flow again, but got stuck around the Floozy's belly and panicked.

"Woe is me," wailed The Dress, "I tried cascading . . . I am supposed to underscore the curve, but you have no arse." The reactions of The Dress were getting more British and more vulgar by the minute.

"Pull yourself together," barked The Floozy, but The Dress was inconsolable.

"Supposed to cascade …" it howled. "Stifled in the waist … no curve … can't flow … woe is me, woe is me."

Sniveling and yowling, it grasped at the Floozy's front, holding tight at the belly for a few revealing seconds until a hefty pinch made it realize that it was violating The Dress credo of modesty—the wearer of the Dress was to show every curve, but appear demurely clothed at all times. Clinging to the sensitive parts of the body like a wet tee-shirt contest was totally unacceptable.

The waist was pulled so tight at that point that The Dress lost all hope and, with that, all dignity.

"Can't flow," blubbered The Dress in a panic, "I'm not supposed . . . your waist should not fit so tight, that's vulgar!"

"Pull yourself off me," hissed the Floozy, but The Dress was in a full-on identity crisis.

"Can't breathe! My fibers are thinner than human hair, and there's still no air for me! Your thick waist! What do I do?! I'm the real deal, my pedigree impeccable . . . why did you buy me? What's the idea? We do not belong together! It's against my very nature, I cannot breathe!"

The Dress was clearly losing it and getting spiteful.

"Shut up," snarled The Floozy, "Enough with your pedigree and your cost; you are bought and paid for! Now cut it out and do your job."

The Dress sobbed and, full of shame, tried to hide between The Floozy's knees, scrunched itself in a V-shaped wrinkle and began creeping up her legs muttering something that sounded very much like "wankers."

"Why is she pinching herself between her legs and muttering to herself?" The Raccoon turned his rhetorical question to Mrs. Grimm, but, "Where did our client disappear . . . when??" he re-addressed that part to Hoppy.

"Gone. Moves like a snow leopard," confirmed Hoppy, whose only job was to watch the courtroom with eagle eyes.

"You didn't think to stop her?"

"Like a snow le. . ."

"Shut up and fetch her. The court's reconvening!" demanded The Raccoon.

Still stuck in the mousetrap, I did not actually see all of this, and one should never take The Raccoon's word on unfettered faith, but this is what, *I am told*, happened next. The stray Mr. Grimm walked back in the courtroom, looked around like he saw the world for the first time, and crossed the isle between two camps. Walking in brisk stride, he headed for the right side, our side.

In the middle of the third bench back from the counsel table, Mr. Grimm stopped, took off his jacket, folded it inside out, and carefully placed it on the bench, as though he was staking out a spot. This seemed superfluous because the courtroom was empty except for Hoppy who was watching the pantomime with widening eyes and The Raccoon, who sensed responsibility and started to panic.

"Is he sitting down behind us?"

Hoppy nodded.

"Is he with us now? Do we represent him too?"

A gentle tap on the head made him jump.

"I'm Mr. Grimm, your client's husband" said Mr. Grimm, "Please tell your boss this case was settled. We are going home now." He did not move, however, waiting for a response with his shoulders squared at The Raccoon.

"Who's the 'we'," The Raccoon tried to buy some time. Mr. Grimm was much more imposing up close.

"My *wife*," said Mr. Grimm, emphasizing "wife" with the flair of a much more conservative man, "will be expecting a full refund . . . just imagine all the nastiness you people dragged her into . . .." Mr. Grimm halted and hissed pejoratively: ". . . alienation of affection."

"Affections. With an "s." Plural," corrected The Raccoon on autopilot.

———————

Mr. and Mrs. Grimm boarded the elevator together and left the courthouse holding hands, without once glancing in the direction of the former mistress, who was still slinking to her side of the courtroom, now looking ten years older.

Back at the office, my little team assembled for our version of what hospitals call M&M, a post-court review of errors and issues.

"They want the money back," I reported to The Management. "The case could not be won, and I had told you so."

"But we did win!" protested The Raccoon.

"What did we win?" inquired The Management.

"We did not lose," corrected Hoppy.

"We won her Husband back," The Raccoon insisted. "That was our mission, and we accomplished it!"

"How?"

Nobody knew how exactly it happened, but both Hoppy and The Raccoon loudly wanted to have us be the winners.

To stop the chaotic racket, I said: "Does anybody know what in the world possessed Mr. Grimm?"

That stopped the chatter only for a heartbeat.

"He saw the mistress in full light," declared The Raccoon. "That dress was never meant to go with her body shape. The woman clearly is stupid. The vulgarity!"

The Management gave him a look.

"What? I have sisters," he defended.

"Eight percent chance," echoed Hoppy, who always likes to talk in numbers.

"A chance of what?"

"Only eight percent of women are hourglass-shaped."

The Raccoon rolled his eyes, but Hoppy would not let up: "There was a University Study. In Carolina. West Carolina? One of those Carolinas, anyway. Or maybe one of the Dakotas?"

"Are we refunding the money?" asked the Management, voicing the only question that mattered.

Mrs. Grimm had paid joyously, but the chance she would now renege and demand a refund was getting quite real. If she asked what we had accomplished for her, I wasn't quite sure how to answer convincingly.

"Don't spend it yet," I said. "Leave it in her trust account."

Nothing gets a lawyer in trouble with the State Bar as quickly as a fee dispute involving money already in the lawyer's hands. Mrs. Grimm's twenty-five thousand dollars still parked in my trust account were not nearly worth losing my license to practice.

The Grimm Trial Victory was filed under "tactically unclear and fiscally quite questionable." The Raccoon resented the designation and pointed to the first meeting's transcript: "She asked to get her husband back. And he *is* back. We got him back. Am I the only one who wants a bonus?"

THE PORTRAIT BY FRANK COVINO

A WEEK LATER, Mr. and Mrs. Grimm celebrated their newly found appreciation for each other by hosting an exquisite but intimate dinner party. The rack of lamb was served with fresh figs from the garden. The peaches, flown specially from Lane Southern Orchard in Georgia were served fresh, sprinkled with the South Carolina honey.

"It will be a re-commitment party," explained Mrs. Grimm to Mr. Grimm, gently adjusting her husband's tie. "So that everybody *knows* we are together again, but we do not have to spell it out for them."

As usual, Mrs. Grimm knew exactly how to tactfully engage local society. The party would quietly put in the know everybody who mattered. The men who were invited to the party came with their wives, but they were not entirely the Grimms' usual party crowd.

Al Snipes, the head manager of the country club which Mr. Grimm used to frequent before the separation ended Mr. Grimm's privileges, was the first one to greet the prodigal husband with genuine assurance. "My friend, where have you been all year, dear chap? . . . What do you mean subscription lapsed? . . . That's a mistake. That'll be fixed at once . . . I'll see you on the tennis courts at eight sharp tomorrow." The day when Al had two of his Security goons escort Mr. Grimm off the club property apparently escaped Al's memory. It was the same day when Mrs. Grimm had changed the locks on the marital house, so Mr. Grimm remembered that day vividly . . . but today, this evening, he was grateful to forget and to look forward to the game of tennis.

The next guest—Will Johnson, head of a private banking entity—assured Mr. Grimm that there had *never* really been a freeze on the joint accounts, and that Mr. Grimm was welcome to use the money any time. "Any time, the petty cash is at your complete disposal, mate, here's the card." The day when Will ushered Mr. Grimm into the back office and cut his bank card in three jagged pieces on their way to the shredder was to all appearances forgotten.

There were other important men, all clearly suffering from low-grade retrograde amnesia regarding Mr. Grimm's past year's descent from their graces, and they were each and every one manifestly delighted to shake Grimm's welcoming hand, even to clap him on the back in comradely fashion.

The wives of these important guests assured Mr. Grimm that he was "oh so missed" at their last season's parties. Why didn't he RSVP? They worried so when they hadn't heard from him! The invitations must have gotten lost in mail, it was decided, a mutually agreed polite subterfuge in which nobody really believed. For this Season, the mistake regarding the wayward invitations would be corrected straight away. Mr. Grimm was their friend again, and they were all duly enchanted.

Yes, Mr. Grimm was back to playing at his club, in charge of his discretionary funds, and the envy of his clubmates at the parties. Gone were the days of looming uncertainty and fear of poverty. Mrs. Grimm's vast fortune was back at Mr. Grimm's service and, as absence is said to make the heart grow fonder, he was fonder of the status quo more than ever before.

The evening ended pleasantly, inside by the grand fireplace, now flickering only with candles that the maid lit as a seasonal adaptation for the warm weather gatherings. The women, exhausted by the excitement, chatting among themselves; men contentedly sipping the last drink of the evening. The past few months had disappeared, vanished from the collective memory. Gone. Mrs. Grimm was always so good with these social things. Mr. Grimm was so lucky to have her.

How could he think to give up this bliss?
How could he ever get tired of this?

In the quiet bliss of the evening, Mr. Grimm tried to remember what foolishness had possessed him. His life was so pleasantly planned in this house—the boardroom meetings, the charity balls, the special evenings with his attractive, elegant wife. He knew his life's schedule months ahead. Like a celebrity or political figure. As years floated by, he had started to feel irrelevant, replaceable, a cog in the machine of Mrs. Grimm's Life Plan. He was told where to go, what to wear, what to say. "Like a soldier," he had complained to himself. He had grown restless. Nothing he did mattered, and nothing he could do would matter. He felt dead.

And then there was the girl . . . he did not want to even think her name now. Thinking another woman's name would be disloyal to Martha. With him, it was never about an attraction to another woman. He never was the type to cheat on his wife. What it was . . . The girl *needed* him. He mattered to her. He could change the course of a life. He felt alive. Powerful. He'd help that poor girl to get out of the slums. He would have dragged a human being out of desperate poverty, he would have re-made a person. He would have mattered. His escapade was not, he reasoned to himself, a case of thinking with one's gonads but, rather, merely a (perhaps over-generous) response to his innate sense of *noblesse oblige.*

In a very real manner, the whole misunderstanding was all Mrs. Grimm's fault, he decided. She was so graceful, so tactful, so set on the image: *Mr. and Mrs. Grimm.*

He was part of the "Mr. *and* Mrs. Grimm" power couple for so long that it was an honest surprise to discover just "Mr. Grimm."

What was he thinking? Mr. Grimm could not help a soul! Though with only the noblest of intentions, he had been wrong to think that he could help Floozy. Instead, that wretched girl was dragging him down, away from his erstwhile blissful regime of meticulously scheduled days. Having learned an embarrassing lesson, he now just wanted to play his part in Mr.-and-Mrs.-Grimm!

It was such a relief in that courthouse, when the lawyers were out of the way, and he got down on his knee right in the empty courtroom, and asked for his wife's forgiveness, and she said she would try. And he had cried real tears.

Thank God, he was allowed back.

Mr. Grimm gazed happily around his newly reacquired sitting room. Above the mantel, his wife's grand portrait by the brilliant Italian Frank Covino caught his eye. He'd seen this oil hundreds of times before, and just as many times the "Portrait of Madame X" from whom Covino clearly pinched the pose. The portrait was on the cover of Duck Vogue, and all that month Martha was "the lady in the Dress," and he was proud because young girls would stop his wife asking her to autograph the cover.

"*You can grow up even more beautiful,*" she would write across the cover. For every one of her admirers, no matter how plain or poor. Martha was kind. He could not stop a fond smile.

But now there was something both newly familiar and yet fresh about the oil. In the portrait, Mrs. Grimm stood in full length, her right hand pushing away the surface of a coffee table, her body twisted to the left, as though she heard a sound from behind her left shoulder. What was so fresh about the portrait? At once, it hit him.

"My dear, can you remember the dress you wore to pose for the portrait?"

Mrs. Grimm's eye flickered with wicked joy. "Cool

wool," she said, "It was all the rage in Britain that Spring, the *elegant allure*."

He loved the way she rolled the "l"s.

"That Dress is what got my portrait onto the Duck Vogue cover," she beamed a self-deprecating smile. Then she smiled wider, in open and unabashed amusement: "Is that where that silly young girl got the idea?"

THE EPILOGUE

THE LETTER DID not come by regular mail. It was hand delivered, but boldly placed in the mailbox amid the routine medley of proclamations of hatred and war penned by opposing lawyers and contending for space among the glossy magazines printed by various lawyers' organizations filled with resolutions to live a clean life, respect each other and bathe amicably in the warm sea of professional courtesy. This particular letter stood out—and not just because it was the only piece that flagrantly violated the statute 18 United States Code §1725, and Post Office Regulations pursuant thereto, providing that stamped letters are protected from the shameful indignity of having to share their mailbox with "any matter not bearing postage."

The envelope was heavy cotton with geometric shades in subdued gold. I had encountered this pattern before, but could not quite place it, not at first. I went to the kitchen and mindfully opened it with the grapefruit knife, along the top. The paper inside was in the same heavy cotton paper stock as the envelope, matching in gold geometrical pattern on one side, except that the ornate tracing vanished at the edge of a blank writing space where Mrs. Grimm had inscribed a short message in her firm cursive handwriting:

My Dear Portia,

I received a letter from your Manager about my account. Please give her my apology and use my funds you hold in trust to settle all invoices.

I queried Mr. Grimm and he confirms making an unfortunate comment to your . . . raccoon, was it? You must forgive my sweet Mr. Grimm—he always is so protective of me, and is not always tactful. But please assure your people that I have no gripe with any of your bills. It was money well spent.

I was interrupted by a rustle.

"From Mrs. Grimm? What did she say?" The Raccoon had materialized out of nowhere and was sniffing the envelope quizzically.

"Yes, it's from Martha Grimm," I explained somewhat redundantly. "She writes to tell us she will not dispute the bill. It turns out, she thinks that she was perfectly served."

"We get a bonus?" Ever-the-optimist, The Raccoon gave the empty envelope a shake, as if to dislodge a hidden treasure, and, finding none, went on lyrically, "I just knew Mrs. Grimm would come through!"

"How big-hearted of Mrs. Grimm," The Management, appearing as she does at the merest mention of money, had already somehow taken possession of the envelope, pinched it by the corner and lifted to her eye-level. "Better late than never. In the same spirit of generosity, I won't squeal to the Feds about her hand-delivered letter's violation of the sanctity of the mailbox."

One can generally count on The Management to always see the worst in people.

39215639R00087

Made in the USA
San Bernardino, CA
21 September 2016